Country

Country

A Novel

MICHAEL HUGHES

CUSTOM
HOUSE

COUNTRY. Copyright © 2019 by Michael Hughes. All rights reserved.
Printed in the United States of America. No part of this book may be
used or reproduced in any manner whatsoever without written
permission except in the case of brief quotations embodied in critical
articles and reviews. For information, address HarperCollins
Publishers, 195 Broadway, New York, NY 10007.

HarperCollins books may be purchased for educational, business,
or sales promotional use. For information, please email the Special
Markets Department at SPsales@harpercollins.com.

Originally published in the United Kingdom in 2018 by John Murray
(Publishers), an imprint of Hachette UK.

FIRST U.S. EDITION

Library of Congress Cataloging-in-Publication Data
has been applied for.

ISBN 978-0-06-294032-2

19 20 21 22 23 LSC 10 9 8 7 6 5 4 3 2 1

for Enda and Denis

Crisis

1

Fury. Pure fury. The blood was up. Lost the head completely.

Achill, the man from the west. The best sniper the IRA ever seen. All called him Achill, but his name was plain Liam O'Brien. After the da, Big Liam O'Brien, who came out of Achill Island and bore the name before him. So the son was called Achill in his turn, though he was born and reared in Castlebar and he'd never set foot in the place, for the da always said it was a fearful hole.

What was the start of it? The whole wrecking match, that sent so many strong souls roaring down to hell, dogs chewing up the guts ground into the road, birds pecking at the splattered bits of their brains. The way London wanted it to go. The way it always is.

Here's what. Pig and Achill fell out. The OC and the trigger man. Bad, bad news.

And whose fault was that? Here's who. One particular Prod farmer from up the country, a man all knew as Crisis Cunningham, who owned the land where they were prepping the job, that Pig had been renting since the ceasefire was called. Ninety-six, this was, the year just turned. The farmer motored down to get back his daughter, for the girl had disgraced him by running away and flinging herself at Pig, after he called in to the house to settle his account the week before. She was shacked up now at his place, doing his washing, cooking his dinner. Whatever else.

So this man Cunningham sent word to Pig and his brother Dog, and he was told to come on down to the farm for a wee chat. The whole squad gathered to hear, round the side of the barn, ducked in under the jut of the roof in case a chopper went over. Stamping away the cold, puffing into their hands.

The old man said his piece, laid it all out. The whole recitation of his credentials and bona fides. No interest in politics of any colour or creed, you pays your money and no questions asked. But he knew better than to frig around with lads the like of them. He hadn't come empty-handed, no sir. A bag full of cash for Pig, big bundles of sterling twenties, English notes. The keys to his own Merc. The promise of a prize bull, once the next season was done, worth ten or twelve grand itself.

Then it started. The man begged, he plain begged for the young one back, weeping and whining, down on his knees in the wet dung of the yard. 'She's hardly fourteen, the light of my life. Please don't touch her, big man. Not yet a while. Give her a couple more years to be a wee girl. I buried her mother and my mother both this past year. The heart is already tore out of me. I can't stand losing the last bit of joy I have.'

Nobody knew where to look. It would scunder you to see a grown man like yon choking on his sobs and snotters. They all nudged other, and the mutter went round. 'Go on there, Pig, let the girl go back home with her da, and we'll have no more said about it.'

Not Pig. He laughed his big dirty laugh, right in the poor man's face. 'Away and shite. I take no orders from muck-savage Orange bastards. The girl stays where she is, and she'll be doing my ironing and plenty besides till her pubes turn grey, if I want her to. Now get to fuck out of this before you're carried out.'

He drew his short, snapped off the safety. And away the old man skedaddled, hoofing it down the back lane at a fair old lick.

But the minute he got in home, he lifted the phone to a certain individual. 'You know I take no sides,' he says, 'and I never ask for nothing. But family is family, and I bring in the vote for you here in the townland every election. So this one time, there's a wee favour you can maybe do for me.'

2

Next thing, the power was off at the farm. And the phone. No sign of anything tampered with. No problems anywhere else. One of them things. Sit it out.

The day after, the water too. When they went to head out to see what was what, a patrol was spotted nearby, rooting around in the bushes. They had to duck back in and lie low, couldn't take the risk. Word came up that it wasn't safe below in the town either. The place was suddenly crawling with Brits and peelers, and every one of them lads was on the list. Pig made it known they were to stay out of sight, no matter what. No exceptions.

Fucked, every man jack of them. Stuck on that wee farm up the back of beyond. No plan B neither. Nobody knew they were there, do you see. They daren't send word to the local Shinners, for fear it might leak out what they were scheming at. Petrol nearly done. Fags running low. The mobile phones out of juice. Rationing the Calor. Three days. Four. Living on stale biscuits and mouldy bread. Hoking through the bins for any oul bit of real grub. Drinking dregs of rainwater. Half of them sick as dogs by the end of the week. Puking up their rings, sweating and raving.

Sitting around in the wet and the cold of the barn and the rotten old house, the boys were at the end of their rope. Time to call off the job and get out of this forsaken shithole, steal away to America to disappear for good. The old talk came back now, of giving up the whole armed struggle as a bad job. It had been going nowhere fast this long time. Cash out and let the fucking Shinners jaw their way to the table, good luck to them.

Pig stayed out of it, away in the back room with his young one. Nobody knew what he thought. Nobody dared go near him.

Achill couldn't stick it. He took the chance, went up that evening to the box at the crossroads and phoned down to the parochial house. There was a tame curate below he knew could be relied on. The priest said he'd make some enquiries, get to the bottom of things, head up the next day and fill them in. Achill told him he'd be met at the top of the lane and driv up to the farm.

He got all the lads together in the barn, first thing. Dog, Sid, Budd and the Other Jack, Macken, Merrion and old Ned. Pig too, still in a sulk. Sitting there squinting at Achill, saying not a damn thing. The Superser was lit and the kettle on the camping stove and the last of the Jammie Dodgers laid out, the full treatment. They lit their fags and waited. Not a peep out of one of them. Just waiting.

The priest showed up, on the dot. He'd been searched first, then a spud sack over his head and hid down in the back of the car, a blanket across him. Knew exactly where he was heading, but never said a word. He'd done the like a dozen times.

Led into the barn, the spud sack lifted away. Nipping

pickles of muck off his jumper, nodding and smiling, hemming and hawing.

'Now, boys. Before I begin. I'm here as a man of God and a man of peace, to pass on a message and nothing else, and before I do, I want a solemn promise that neither me nor my church will be touched if it's news that's not welcome, either now or in years to come. There are some here present who are known to lose the head when things go agin them, or if they don't, then to hold a grudge till they find a quiet wee time to pay it off, and I want none of that nonsense.'

'I'll guarantee your peace,' says Achill. 'No fucker, beg your pardon, Father, no bastard here will go near you, not now nor never, so long as I'm alive, even if it's the boss man himself you lay the blame at.'

'A good spake,' says the priesteen. 'And I'll hold you to it, for he's the very one.'

Well. The loudest silence ever you heard. Like the air itself was sucked out of the place. All eyes went to the floor, nobody dared steal a glance nor half a glance at Pig.

'That man Crisis Cunningham,' says the priest, 'who owns this land we're standing on, and came down here looking his daughter back. You all know he's a Protestant. And it seems he's been in contact with a certain politician on the other side of the house that you know and that I know, and who happens to be married to a second cousin of his. A man by the name of Mr Paul Bright. Yes, him. No specifics mentioned, but that man has been asked to pull a few strings, get your water cut off and your power cut off. The security forces told there might be something afoot in the local area, and now you daren't stir abroad. It looks like you picked the wrong man to pee off. Unless it's settled pretty damn quick, he'll spill the beans entirely, is my own opinion, and you'll be lifted by the RUC in short order, rotting in the Maze for the next twenty years, or else filling up the graveyard before your time like so many of your old compadres, if the army gets wind of what you're about, ceasefire or no.'

Shitting themselves now. All eyes looked to Pig, but Achill got in first. 'Don't be shy, Father. Work away. What have we to do?'

'My personal advice,' says the priest, 'is to take the girl back to the da quick march. Accept nothing off him, but send her home with any cash money you can gather, good clothes, make-up, records, whatever she wants and you can lay your hands on. Get back in the good books as soon as you can, any way you can, and then he'll call off the dogs, that's the message I was told. Nothing political, nothing sectarian, just a small personal matter. Your OC there is the only man to blame. Nobody else.'

Well if you'd seen Pig. Rared up and flung his chair at the wall. Toe to the table and Jammie Dodgers flying everywhere. Waste of good biscuits. Tea as well, he near scalded his own brother Dog. Everybody bit their lips and sat tight. Because, what else do you do?

And if you'd heard him. Guldering and gurning. Gnashing and spitting. Rounding on the lot of them.

'The fuck is this shite? A fucking Jaffa sending a fucking

priest down here to tell me where to point my fucking prick? Every volunteer among us has a young thing on the go, and that's his right as a man on the run, and as a soldier of destiny kept away from his home place night after night while he's fighting hard for his nation. And now I've to give up mine? Well it's not fair lads, it's not fucking fair! I'm fond of that girl. And she's cracked on me. If I'd to choose, I'd take her over my own wife, any day of the week! I tell you this. Priests never bring good news. Never have, never will. The Catholic Church is a blight on the Irish people, worse than the fucking Brits! I curse the black day St Patrick came ashore in this country!'

That took the lid off. The lot of them all started in now, waving their arms and shouting other down.

Pig smacked his blackthorn on the tin wall, rap rap rap, shut them all back up.

'Would youse let me finish, to fuck! Can a man not let off a bit of smoke without a crowd of oul women start yabbering round him!

'So.

'Listen up.

'Fair or not, I know the score. If it's for the good of these men and the good of the cause, then you'll get no argument from me. Back she goes to her fucking da.'

Well, the looks of them. Like bold children you'd just told that Santy was coming after all.

And that should have been the end of it. They would have gone to their beds happy, and all concerned would be alive today to tell their own tale.

No such luck. This is Pig we're talking about. 'But I'll tell youse what else.' And there was whisht again. 'No way am I doing without. Away off now and find me another, and look smart about it.' That wiped the stupid smiles off their gobs. 'You hear confessions, Holy Joe, you know well who the Provie sluts are in this here place, the ones that cream their knickers every time a Brit gets plugged. I want names and addresses, wrote out. Hair colour, size of tits, what school, the ma and da and the whole connection. When the heat's off I'll drive around and scope them out, make my choice. And when I have, you may go down yourself and bring the glass slipper.'

My God. If you'd seen the goes-ons of the priest. Hopping and stammering. Sweating like a sow. And the men no better.

All looked to Achill. None other dared a word, not even Dog.

'Well houl on, Pig,' says Achill, raising his hands, easy enough, only making a point. 'Houl on there one wee second, just. No entanglements in the local area, you know the form. Word gets about, people ask questions, stick their noses in. We're to lie low, draw no attention. Now, once we're finished our business, it's a different story. You can have any girl you want that time. Line them up and take your pick. When this here job is done, they'll be flinging themselves at you. Three and four at a time, if you want them. Don't you worry, there'll be no shortage of easy women after.'

Pig stood his ground, laughed his hard oul laugh again.

'Typical devious backhanded talk out of you, Achill. Connaughtmen are all the same. You get to keep your piece while I have to do without? No fucking way. If there isn't a girl to be had round here, then I'll just have to requisition Sid's girl off him, or Budd's. Aye, or why not your own wee Brigid?'

Achill. The face on him.

But Pig wised himself up, turned his back. Kept the head. He could when he needed to.

'No more rowing in front of the stranger,' says Pig. 'Time enough for that. There's serious business here. Sid, Achill, some of you, take that young one of mine back to her fucking da, say what needs to be said. Get us back up and running by first light tomorrow, or I'll want to know why not.'

'You treacherous, backstabbing cunt,' says Achill.

The mercury dropped a few more degrees. Nobody moved a muscle. Nobody took a breath.

They'd all been waiting on the like. This one was coming a while.

Oh, the blood was up now. The famous fury boiling in his belly. You could near hear it.

'Say that again,' says Pig. Real cool and calm, keeping his powder dry.

'Pig by name,' says Achill, 'and pig by nature. Stubborn as you're filthy.' He spat, and stepped round Pig, facing him now, toe to toe, nose to nose. 'I say it to your ugly phiz, once and for all. You're not fit to lead this squad. You're nothing but a crooked oul culchie hoor, same as the rest.

Thinking of nothing and nobody except yourself, your wallet, and your dick. And here you prove it in the sight of all. How is any soldier of Ireland meant to take orders from a self-centred ignorant fat coward like you?'

That was the priest out the door.

Nobody else so much as twitched. All knew the two of them were carrying. This might go any way at all.

'The fuck are you whingeing about now?' says Pig, soft as you like. 'Did Mammy forget to change your nappy?'

'You say you'll take my girl away,' says Achill, 'and I tell you plain, I won't have it. My own wee girl, who came after me, of her own free will, because of what I done. Yes, what I done! Not what you done! I'm the trigger man! I'm the one any decent Irish girl wants to ride, plain and simple! Your skanky wee bitch only hangs round you because you hang round me, that's the truth you can't face hearing!'

And that was him off the lead. No road back. That man had no reverse.

'You'll do exactly as I order you,' says Pig, 'and you'll say Thank You Sir at the end of it.'

'I'll tell you what else,' says Achill, the fury flowing free in him now. 'I'm the one getting blood on my hands in this here squad, and a life sentence hanging over my head! I'm the one that's kept the Brits off these roads this nine long years, shiteing themselves in case the Border Sniper gets them! I'm the one that means the peelers won't come within a hound's gowl of us, for fear of the same! And all through them nine long years, any time we done over a post office or a bookies, you reported a half the amount and kept the most of the haul for yourself! You'll tell me every OC does the same, and the men are glad to get what they get. And I'm not arguing that. But what's given me is mine! What little comes my way from this shitty way of life, I mean to keep a hold of! And now you say you'll take the girl off me, do you? And I'm supposed to sit here like a child and take that, am I? Two words for you. Just. Try. And while I'm at it, here's two more. Fuck. You. Up your yellow fucking hole.'

The pair of them. The eyes of them.

'But do you know what else again?' says Achill. Over at the men now. Changing up to top gear, on the home straight. 'Fuck this here shite! Do ye hear me? Fuck the whole lot of you! This isn't my fight, and it never was!' Scarlet with the fury, practically spitting fire. 'Oh, it's well known what we're really doing here! Sure the dogs in the street know it, that's the great laugh, even if he's kept ye crowd of gombeens in the dark. Well I'm not afraid to speak it out. I'm afraid of no man, and if I was, it wouldn't be him. So listen up.'

Oh, this was trouble. This was crossing a line. But not a one budged till they saw what way the wind would blow.

And besides, nobody wanted to miss a word. However the thing fell out at the heel of the hunt, this would keep them going for months. Years, maybe.

'Ye all got the same word I did, one by one, scattered far and all that we were since the truce was called. Gear up the old squad, prep a big bang and end this here ceasefire. Tell the Brits they've pushed us as far as we can go. Pig made his case, and others like him, and the higher-ups called it. Enough is enough, and we're the boys they picked to do the deed, as soon as we get the nod from Belfast. Pile the pressure back on the Brits, and bomb our way to the table. Blast them out of this green country once and for all.

'Shite, plain and simple. This here operation is no tactical use of the armed struggle, making sure the Shinners get the most they can out of the talks. This here is pure personal vendetta, dirty country shite and not a damn thing to do with uniting this land. Pull all the long faces you want, Dog, but stand up and tell me that's not true bill, and I'll call you a liar to your ugly fucking face.

'Do you not wonder, all of ye, why you were called back in, instead of using clean skins? Every man of us is a red light, some way or other. On the list, or on the run. But Pig wanted to swing his dick, and show off his pull, so here we all are, the cream of the crop, hiding like rats, risking our hides, for nothing but that man's pride.

'The wife left you, isn't that right, Dog? Just upped and away. And the word is, she's been screwing a Brit. Yes, a fucking Brit. You came crying to your big brother, and he went buck mental. The family name in tatters, him a laughing stock from here to Crossmaglen. Caring about nothing save his own fat self.

'So he ordered this squad back in business to pull the plug on these talks and this ceasefire, and fling the whole country back into the dark old days, for no other reason than to get back at that there Brit, and every other Brit that thinks they can walk all over us. Teach them to come sniffing round our women. And then she'll see what fearless warriors the pair of ye are, and she'll come scampering on back to her darling hubby. Just like in the movies.'

The face of Dog. Pure beetroot. The rest with gobs hanging open. Still Achill kept on.

'But here's what, Dog. No, just you stand your ground till I've said my piece. I don't blame you one bit for wanting to get even. Not one wee bit. A man's a man, and you have to do what you have to do.

'But listen here to me. Personal is personal. You can leave me out of it.'

He took a few steps back and showed them his two palms, up over his head, like a priest doing the consecration, or a TV robber about to get cuffed.

'Hear me now, for I say this to all of ye. That Brit never done nothing on me. And I'll tell you better than that. No Brit never done nothing on me. And if they had, then boo hoo, too fucking bad. A war is a war, and both sides have to do many's the dirty doing to get the job done.

'But don't expect me to wipe up your mess. I fight for Ireland alone, not for Dog and his bitch. I pull my trigger for a thirty-two-county republic, not for bogman score-settling.

'And do you know what else? Good for the young one, if you ask me. She has the right idea. Get out away from this fucking shower, and out away from this fucking hole. For that's what I have a mind to do now. Head back west, to my own people, where at least I get a bit of respect for who I am and what I done in my time.

'Armed struggle for Ireland is one thing, but you won't get me fighting another man's fight, to save his own rotten pride. Enough is enough. Right here is where I call it a day. I'm ceasing my fire, and decommissioning my weapons. There.'

He pulled the short out of the back of his trousers, and dropped it on the straw in front of them.

Tumbleweeds isn't even near it. Nobody had the balls to think a thought, never mind speak a word, before Pig himself had his say.

He let them all sweat a good minute, maybe two. Knowing rightly he was doing it, just out of pure badness. Then he spat, and laughed his ugly oul laugh. The words came flying out of him.

'Good riddance,' he says. 'You'll not get me begging you to stay, if that's what you're fishing for. I shed no tears if you want to sulk off, for there's no room in this here outfit for back-seat drivers. Anybody trying to boss me will soon get a rude awakening.

'You think you're so smart, talking out of your hole about our target and our tactics, and proving only that you know sweet fuck all about nothing. As far as I'm concerned, any individual that gets in bed with the enemy is a traitor to their country, be it my own brother's woman, or the West Brit Shinner suits and ties. But it makes no difference what this operation's for and what it isn't for. What I say goes in this unit, and that's the only way to run a military organisation.

'So you're the great hero with blood on your hands? You

done the operations that got us where we are today? So fucking what? Every man to his own. Them jobs were planned and run by volunteers with brains you'll never have. Men like Sid here, the greatest schemer in the whole of the Ra. But he gets no credit from me for doing exactly what he loves doing, nor neither do you. And you love nothing more than putting dirty great holes in a man's skin from half a mile away and watching the blood leak out of him and the life with it. So get away to hell out of this if you want. Whatever suits yourself. No loss, we'll do just fine.

'But I tell you this. I'm coming round to your place tonight, and that wee girl of yours is coming back with me, and that's where she's staying. End of. And you and Pat can get back to your good old bum-chum ways. Pair of fucking queers that you are.'

Well Pig was right about one thing anyway. Achill loved to kill, when he thought it deserved, and for one gorgeous minute he was ready to pick up his short and put a dirty great hole between Pig's two eyes, and let's see the face on him then. Watch the rotten oul brains bubbling down his fat red snout. They can do what they like to me, thought Achill, but I tell you what, that picture would keep me warm in a cold H-Block cell for many's the year.

Except Achill knew he'd never get the length. He was very well aware how that story ended. He'd always known in his soul that his cards were marked, right from the very day he took the oath. But he was fucked if today was going to be the day, and this man the cause. So.

'The day you have Brit blood on your hands,' says Achill,

'is the day you can tell me what's what. The day you do yourself what you ask these men to do, put your own life up for grabs, deep in the hard country with the SAS on your tail baying for blood, is the day I take my next order from you, for I know well you never have in your puff.

'But I promise you this, by all that's holy, cross my heart and hope to die. The day will come, and very fucking soon, when you'll be standing here like that Prod farmer, on your knees in the muck and the glar, begging me to come back, the tears tripping you.

'And I tell you now straight, I won't do it. These men will be lifted out from under you, informers every turn-around, fine volunteers shot down and blown to bits in the road because the Brits aren't frightened to take you on any more, for you've no Border Sniper to hide behind. And I'll be laughing. Fuck, yes. I'll be laughing my hole off. Until the day them same Brits are south of the border, marching in my own land, I won't lift another finger against them. You're on your own.'

The only sound was the crows cawing. Still no man dared be the first to shift.

Until old Ned. Seventy-five if he was a day. He got up on his hind legs now, and that was no small job, for they all knew better than to try and help him. But you could have cut the air with a spade while he struggled off the wee stool, and got up his phlegm. And then he barked out at the pair of them.

'Children! A pair of children squabbling over jubes! I was born when this whole island was still ruled by the

British Empire! I was on operations when you men were sucking bottles of milk, aye, and when some of your mammies and daddies were sucking bottles of milk! I pulled triggers in the Border Campaign in the fifties alongside men who'd fought in the GPO. I was moving families being burned out of their houses in Belfast in sixty-nine, and I brought the first weapons into the Bogside in the back of my own bread van. I was among the heads they came and asked in eighty-one whether to keep on with the hunger strike, or throw in the towel. And now I've had the Army Council drive up and ask me one by one whether to banjax these talks, or let the Shinners have their head. And all them volunteers listened to my spake then, when I had something to say, so you pair better scrape out your lugs and listen to me now.' And they did.

'Achill. Nobody argues you've bagged your share of Brits, and more than your share, and it's thanks to you and nobody else that our whole place is a no-go zone for them and the peelers both. Any man disputing that would be a laughing stock. But you don't go against the OC's orders. You just don't do it. This man here was put in charge for a reason. Wise the fuck up, and calm the fuck down.

'Pig. Let Achill keep his girl. She went after him, not you, and that's just the way it is. Tough shite. We need Achill, you know we do. This whole job is built around his cold eye, and his steady hand, and the fear of God he puts into the Brits. We're royally fucked without him. So do the decent thing, hold up your paws and admit when you're wrong.'

Pig shook his big fat head. 'Good man Ned. Always the right spake at the right time. I can't fault one word of that, but here's the thing. When it's time to debate, we can debate, and argue the bit out, and I'll welcome all views and opinions on that day, nothing held back. But not in the middle of an operation. Not when we're on active service. Active means action, not words, and service means doing what you're told. End of.

'And here's what else. OC means Officer Commanding, and commanding does not mean asking nicely where I come from, it means what the fuck it means. We're fighting a war for a fair and decent democratic republic, but until we get it, we're a cold, ruthless military unit with a simple chain of command, where the boss man's word is law, judge and jury. If any man, never mind who, starts giving orders back up the chain, that's the end of the campaign. We'll fall into feuding like the INLA, is that the story you want? Fighting over drug money? Turning our guns on each other? Digging up gravestones of dead volunteers and fucking them through the front windows of the old men that plugged them, trying to scare them to death? No. However good a shot that man is, however many kills he has chalked up, does that entitle him to show me up in front of everybody, any time he feels like it? If I back down on this, what'll be next? Not an inch, boy. Not now, nor never. I tell you what, the Jaffas are surely right about one thing. No Fucking Surrender is the only way to fight a war.'

'Never a truer word spoke,' says Achill. 'What kind of a man would I be, and what would be said about me by these good men here in years to come, or by others coming after them, if I lay down and let you put your boot on my neck this day? Not me. Not this volunteer. Not now, nor never.

'Easy come easy go, you take the girl. I give her to you. But that's my own decision. And not a button else. Not one red cent of my share are you getting back off me.

'But listen here to me now. If you have a mind to face me down, come on right ahead. I hide from no man. If you're looking a chance to prove to these volunteers that there's red blood instead of pish-water in them veins of yours, then I'm the lad to give them all a good look, right now this very minute. Just say the fucking word, boy.'

And like a scissors cut the string in between, the pair of them heeled off and walked away. Before somebody said something they'd regret, as the man says.

And that was the start of it. A terrible business altogether. Oh, it was all kept off the news, for the sake of the talks and the ceasefire. But them that were around that part of the country remember every bit.

Wait now till you hear the rest.

3

Pig got word to Crisis Cunningham that the wee girl was on her way home, and Sid was sent to bring her in person, with wads of cash and new duds and the whole kit and caboodle, and all the honey his tongue was good for, to smooth things over. The da was all smiles, apologised for the misunderstanding, and any inconvenience caused. He'd get on to Mr Bright straight away and let him know it was a false alarm. All would be just as it was.

But Pig himself wouldn't listen to a soul. Dug the heels right in. He sent two young lads down to Achill's place, hardly more than balloons, with a message for the young one Brigid. There's a vacancy up here and you're to come now and be the OC's girl, for that's the way it was done in them days, and Achill said not a word to them.

'I don't blame ye lads one bit. Do what ye were sent here to do. Pig is the only man my fury holds with.' Pat woke the girl up, told her what was what, and she got herself dressed and went on with a big long face, a wee kiss on the cheek for Achill and that finished him off.

One minute bawling and crying, the next minute red with the rage. Couldn't hardly see, he was that stirred up. Stamping on the ground like he was trying to flatten it. Then he sat in the muck and the dirt, and took the shirt off his back, and tore it into wee strips, like it was a tissue. Mad stuff. Pat tried all sorts, begged and pleaded, but nothing would do him.

Pat, now. You see, Pat owed Achill pretty much everything. They'd shared a cell in the Maze when Achill was in for membership, and Pat for possession, though he was a total innocent, doing a favour for a friend of his that he didn't even know was involved. Anybody could see he was a green gawm, but something about him got to Achill. Maybe he had a glimpse of his own wee self before the whole thing got in round him. And he swore to himself he would take this boy in, for he had nobody else, and put him on the straight and narrow, keep him close indoors and away from Pig and the rest of them, teaching him what was right and what was wrong, same as his own teacher Mannix had him.

Nobody dared say boo to Pat, for fear of Achill's fury. Anybody that tried got their arm in a sling. There was something about that young lad made Achill feel that things were going to work out, one day, that the next lot coming up would find another way through it all, and a better way. He was what they were fighting for. There had to be something.

If Pat was smiling, the sun was out for Achill. And if Pat was in bad form, then you may stay out of Achill's way. That's where the stories started about the two of them, and from them sharing a cell. But the only love between them was one man who needed a big brother, and another man who needed to be one. Brigid was bad enough, but if Pig had laid a finger on Pat, or even threatened to, it would have been High Noon for sure.

But Brigid wasn't the only girl for Achill. As soon as it got dark, straight out the door and up to the box at the crossroads and rang the one number he knew by heart. And fair play to her, she drove up, three in the morning on the wee back roads, and met him.

Theresa Flanagan. A neighbour of Achill's when he first moved north at the age of fifteen, after his da was locked up the first time, and she looked in on him often in them days, washed his clobber, made him his dinner. He had nobody else. Neither did she.

Old enough to be his ma, but in them days she'd give him the odd blow job when he had nothing going on, and he kept the Ra off her back when she was told she'd be tarred and feathered or worse. For all said she was what they used to call a good-time girl. A few quid and she'd do whatever you fancied. But then the Brits got hold of her, so the story went, and the word went round she was working for them too, a honeytrapper, getting the gossip off horny Ra men. Or that there was hidden cameras in her wee house and they'd get pictures of you riding her, to threaten to give your wife or your ma, to try and make you tout.

Achill didn't believe any of it, but he didn't not believe it either. He knew she was in cahoots with the both sides some way or other, he'd always known that. But he knew to say nothing to her, and she knew not to ask. Except the very odd time, if another Ra man was doing his head in, he might mention the name in passing, so the boy would get hassled by the peelers for a couple of weeks, his house and his business done over, the wife strip-searched, car took apart.

So the woman Theresa said she would meet him by the old creamery, and bring him up to a quiet spot she knew. Achill got in the back of the car and she drove before they were seen. He hunkered down with a blanket over him the woman had there for the purpose. The two never spoke till they came to a halt again, up by the reservoir. The woman Theresa had a key and let them in the gate. He locked it behind them, and they drove around behind the pumping station where none could see them but the herons and the gulls.

He turned on the wee light above the seats and handed her a scrap of paper where he had wrote 'TURN OFF THE TAPE OR I WON'T SAY NOTHING'. The pair of them looked at other for a full minute, two, three. Each knew what the other would be saying and was answering every silence by their own silence, and the other knew what that silence was saying too. Not a word out of one of them.

She told him to get out of the car a second, and he did. Then she told him to get back in again and that there was nothing to worry his wee head about now. He said there better fucking not be. And then she sucked his dick.

After, she sat up and he lay down with his head in her lap, the usual. She stroked his hair and said he was her own little boy. He had a quiet wee cry and whispered about his mammy. She didn't mind one bit.

'It's been a fair while,' she says. 'I was wondering what I'd done.'

'I want no backchat,' he says. 'It's a simple matter and I need it dealt with fast.'

'You'll have to fill me in.'

'Fill you in, nothing. I know well you have eyes and ears besides mine.'

'Maybe I have and maybe I haven't. All the same, I want to hear it from your own tongue. I know who I can trust and who I can't. But if you're in any kind of bother, and I can help, just say the word. I owe you plenty, and I pay my debts.'

Nothing for a minute or two.

'The young thing I took up with on the way down. I'm sure you know the one.'

She rooted around in her bag, and handed over a wee square photo. 'Brigid Nealon.'

'Fuck me,' says Achill. 'Where did you get that?'

She laughed. 'It's my own.'

Achill gawped at her. Thinking back everything he'd ever said in front of her.

She laughed again, at the stares of him. 'What did you think I was, just some ha'penny tout?'

Achill took the picture.

'That's her,' says Achill. 'Christ of almighty. Tell me the truth, did you ever see a girl like her? The boys from the class in school. It was said and said again, the only thing could love you is your mother. I fairly showed them. But my ma never loved me, Theresa. The only thing she loved was the drink. I've told you the whole history.'

'Your mother had a hard life.'

'Aye, and she gave me a harder one. I shed no tears for her, whether she's living or dead. But this girl belongs to me. I won her, by my own deeds. That's all there is to it.'

'Except now she's left you.'

'She's been made leave me. That treacherous cunt Pig. Had to give up his own piece, and then said he wouldn't do without, and he'd a mind to take my girl off me. I wouldn't stand for it, and he took it very bad.'

'What did the girl say?'

'Sure, what could she say? She's his girl now.'

'So you want her back, is that it?'

'She can go and jump. I got what I needed out of her. It's him I want a swing at.'

'What good am I to you there?'

'Don't act the innocent, it doesn't suit you. I want that man took down a peg or two. I need him and his whole fucking shower to get a hiding they won't forget in a hurry.'

'There's plenty on both sides wouldn't mind seeing the same boy get a boot up the hole. He's not very popular with some of his own people. I'm sure you know well the higher-ups in Belfast are pushing for the truce to stay in place, and it's Pig and his renegades down here who are pulling the other way. Is he up to some divilment?'

'That's for me to know and you to find out. I won't go into the whys and wherefores. But he needs to know they won't get on too well without Achill. They need a hammering like they've never had with me among them. I want the bit of respect I deserve, that's the long and the short of it. Do whatever you need to do.'

'I never thought I'd see the day. But it just goes to show. Everybody's got their limit.'

'Save it. Just do what you're bid.'

'Anything for my own wee boy. And don't you worry, I'll say nothing.'

'Say what the fuck you like. There's neither chickenshit Brit nor plastic peeler nor Loyal Orange hood will dare take me on. Not even the fucking SAS. They know what I am, and what's waiting on them if they try. And they won't know a thing about it till they see their own red guts splashed out on the road.'

She wondered at him, doing the like of this. But she knew better than to ask.

'Come on here and roll down them seats. You've earned more than your suck job the night.'

4

The minute she was in home, Theresa lifted the phone and called London. First time in three years, and it was somebody new answered, but they trained them well, and once she said a certain name she was put straight through. Another word, and she was transferred to the very top. And I mean the very top.

'I have a wee favour to ask.'

'What do you think you're playing at? Go through the proper channels.'

'Not this time. You owe me. And I expect my debts to be paid, in full.'

She gave him the whole yarn. At the end of it, a big crackly sigh down the phone.

'You know perfectly well that won't wash with Dublin. We can't go in mob-handed while they're on ceasefire. The talks are at a very delicate stage.'

'When are they not? I can help you with that too. For want of a nail, do you remember that one? It's people like me know what's happening on the ground, and I'm telling you, this man Pig is in your road. His people will never accept giving up their guns without a promise of withdrawal, and he has a lot of sway in the area and beyond. You need to get him out of the picture. Worst-case scenario, it's a chance to exert a bit of pressure, the kind they understand. If they start thinking they can't trust their own people, morale goes. Best-case scenario, it ends up with a feud, and they spend the next six months chasing each other round the back hills.'

'Out of the question. Things have moved on since your heyday. We exert no pressure on the local factions. We simply don't get involved. We're honest brokers.'

'Spare me the soundbites. I don't need a politics lecture.'

'Clearly you do. Sinn Fein and Dublin are living in cloud cuckoo land. Both demand a date for withdrawal, and while nothing would give us greater satisfaction than to be rid of the bloody place for good, that's not politically possible, and they know it. We can't move anything through the Commons without the unionists, and their price is decommissioning of weapons before Sinn Fein enters the talks. Stalemate.

'But we're working on both sides, slowly and patiently, inching them closer together. Three steps forward, two steps back. And just when Sinn Fein look like they might want to dance, you're asking for an unprovoked aggression against their people, in the middle of a ceasefire? When they're finally showing the political courage to take their movement by the hand towards a political settlement? By Jove, I don't think so. Not on your nelly.'

'Have you forgot what I done for you?'

Nothing.

'And then maybe you have. So I'll spell it out.

'Remember the time the IRA found out that Bonnie

Prince Charlie was to visit thon school in Dungannon? Aye. And youse got word of the leak, so you pulled the plug. And then you did a second search, and you found a command wire in under the stage of the dinner hall, and the squib ready waiting in a garage down the road. Don't play dumb. Oh, it was kept off the news, but the talk was about.

'Well, it was me who gave you that word. Remember now? Aye. So I'm not nothing. It was said to me on that day, if there was ever anything I needed doing, no matter what, I was to come direct to you. Direct to you. And here I am, calling it in. You owe me big time, is the bottom line. After this, we're quits.

'And don't give me that honest-broker shite. It's your army and your SAS that's been working flat out this twenty years or more to smash the IRA, to smash anybody but your own good selves that's got the gumption to lift a finger to defend themselves and their families and their communities. You don't get to have it both ways, you know. The republicans aren't the only ones have been fighting with the Armalite in one hand and the ballot box in the other. Isn't that right? But nobody's complaining. Your army has to do what your people demand. Keep them safe. Sure that's all you're good for at the end of the day, never mind all the big talk. Spend their silver, and guard the gate. Beyond that, it's just a load of blah blah blah. And the very same with them. That's politics, boyo.

'So just you get on the blower to Dublin, and tell them what's what. Oh, they'll buck and they'll scream and they'll kick their legs, but they don't have your muscle. One clap of thunder out of you, and they'll be quaking in their boots. You just tell them you'll pull the guilt money out of the North, or you'll block their EEC handouts at the next council meeting, or you'll get the Yanks to stick on a few import tariffs they could do without.

'Tell them it's a done deal. London has given it the nod, and once the nod is given, the nod can't be ungiven. Just tell them that.'

5

Pig got woke up by a tap at the front door. On and on and on. He found his watch by the bed. Near two in the morning. Nobody was supposed to know he was back in home.

Up and peeped down out the window. Wee Stevie, the young lad that went back and forth with messages. The fuck did he want? But you never know, it might be something.

Pig opened the door quick and grabbed him.

'Come in here to fuck, before you're seen. Do you not know what time it is?'

'I didn't think you'd be sleeping, there's that much going on.'

'Everybody has to sleep some time. You can die from lack of sleep on its own.'

'Can you?'

'Fuck up and tell me your business, and it better be good.'

Wee Stevie gave Pig the envelope. He told him no more than the truth. He'd been handed this stuff round the back of the Ships by a couple of lads who'd robbed it out of one particular car parked down by the old handball courts. They'd been told to look out for that one particular car, for it was known to be a plain-clothes RUC car, and to nick what they could if it was ever seen sitting empty.

But what Stevie didn't know, and Pig didn't know, was that one of them wee lads had signed up just the other week to feed bits and pieces to Special Branch now and again, to get him off a drugs charge. And he had informed to Special Branch that he was told to look out for this particular car, among a load of other similar shite that he thought could do no harm to anybody. Somebody in the barracks picked it out of the report, and an army plain-clothes lad had come in and told them to put this certain envelope in a very nice leather bag on the passenger seat of that car and leave it parked where it had no business being parked. The two boys were going to be lifted now shortly and given a hiding by the peelers, just in case Pig checked the story out. Which he would.

'It might be nothing,' says Stevie, 'but I thought it looked like something. I've told nobody else, I swear to God.'

Pig handed Stevie a scrunched-up fiver, and then a second one. He was a good lad. Knew when to keep his mouth shut, which was something these days. Scally eye, so he was always eager to please. He'd give him a leg up when he needed it.

'If there's ever anybody giving you bother, you let me know. And don't be shy. Tell them straight out they'll have to answer to the boss man.'

Stevie tightened up his lips and nodded. Pig would have swore he saw the lad grow an inch taller. These things changed you, at the right age. Just a wee nudge.

When the lad was gone, Pig closed the curtains and opened the envelope.

A big thick pile of stuff. Classified all over it. Intelligence assessments, memos and printouts, scribbled notes and photocopies of notes. Stamps and codes he'd never seen.

He felt his stomach gurgling. His hands were trembling. This might be big.

He sat on the bog and had a read.

Strategic vulnerabilities and big-picture repercussions. The base is at its weakest for many years but we do not believe this is apparent to the local community. We are rebuilding a certain section and the warning is that this would be the worst time to have an attack. The place could be taken out once and for all.

Another page.

Our current assessment is that GB public morale is very low and the stomach is no longer there in London and the MOD to continue Operation Banner indefinitely. Politically we are looking for an endgame. We have accepted the inevitability of a united Ireland within a generation, and quite possibly sooner if the temperature changes.

He read on. And on. He could not believe his sleepy wee eyes. He fell for it hook, line and sinker. An old trick, but it hardly ever failed. Leak some dodgy information, have it fall into the wrong hands accidentally-on-purpose, stir the other side up into having a go, and let things roll on from there. Clean hands. Nobody to blame but themselves.

6

Coat on over the jim-jams, in the car and straight up the town, to rouse Ned. On the blower first, to get Dog on the scene too. He sat them both down in the good room at Ned's and handed round the stuff.

'Look at this here. Literally fell into my lap, in the middle of the night. I had to slap myself or I'd have swore the whole thing was a fucking dream. Look at it, would you. It says one big result for us could lead to political pressure in London for a military pull-out, a negotiated settlement that would be reunification in all but name, and fuck the unionists. Dublin has won the argument, it could be done this year or next at the latest, and all it would take is one big blow. The military is weak, they don't have the men. Sub-calibre personnel. Lack of intel. Very vulnerable to attack.

'I'm telling you, boys, it's Christmas morning. We start moving, without delay, and fuck what anybody else says. Fuck Achill. Fuck the talks. Fuck waiting on the nod. The job is on. I'll get word up to Belfast, and they may give it the rubber stamp.'

'If anybody else had brought me a yarn the like of this, I'd have chased them,' says Ned. 'But you're the OC, and your word goes. Let's get the rest of them up.'

Not Pig. Oh no. That was far too simple for him.

'Stall a minute. I want to know first what these boys have left in the tank after eighteen months pipe and slippers. We'll set them a wee test of their mettle. That's the way it was done with me, and they're going to get the same treatment now. Call the lot of them together.'

7

Sid sent out a comm to call a meeting of the usual suspects for that Saturday night, up at the Ships. If anybody asked, they were to say they were there for the parish quiz.

The pub sat right by the border, from long before there was any such thing, and the original wee building in the North had been extended again and again so the most of the premises was now in the South. The Brits knew well that was where they met, but there was fuck all they could do about it. The front bar was their jurisdiction, with prices in sterling, but the rest of the place was out of bounds. As for that side of things, the local gardaí were onside, or paid off, or threatened. They never went near, unless they wanted a pint themselves after hours.

Ten of them got asked, and ten of them were there. Pig sat at the top, with a pile of question cards Sid had wrote out in a hurry, that he could start into in case somebody walked in. Anybody that knew him would see through it in a second, but it would do the trick in a court of law. You could take nothing for granted these days. Touts every-where.

When they heard the bell from the chapel for devotions, Pig stood up, and there was hush. They all pulled in their chairs, and the nod was given to the dickers downstairs.

The music started blaring from below. There was a band on, so nobody would hear a word unless they were right next to Pig. The words came flying out of him.

'*A chairde*. Bad fucking news, and I won't sugar the pill. London's done the dirty on us. I've had documents passed to me from the talks, and they're authentic, I've checked it out with my contacts at Leinster House, and the news is not good. Boys, the story is that the Brits are never going to pull out of Ireland, no matter what. No date for withdrawal, no timetable, no promise it'll be done within a generation. The unionist veto stays in place. Rock solid, cast iron, one hundred per cent. The treacherous cunts! The border is not on the table and it never was. These talks are a sham. And there's not a fucking thing we can do about it.

'To think of the number of them over here, and the number of us! You could set every Brit in the North behind his own bar, each one pulling pints for a pubful of Irish Catholics, and at the end of it you'd still have queues of us with dry tongues hanging out. But they have the loyalists, and the peelers, and the Stoop Down Low Party, all doing their dirty work. The good Protestant Irish, our historic friends and allies for self-determination, deluded and sworn against us. They've strung us along for months and years together, and now we find out the thing is hopeless.

'But here's the crunch. We know we can't defeat them militarily. We've known that this ten years. We could prep a dozen bangs and rip the guts out of bases and towns and cities, here and England both, but I may tell you, if that hasn't worked by now, there's no hope it will. The talks were the only chance, and the armed struggle was the only card we held. But the reality is, our people here on the ground have no more stomach for a fight we can't win. The Brits have us over a barrel.

'So it's time to take a long hard look in the mirror. And though it sticks in my gullet, we need to be men, and stand up and admit the Brits are right. We're done. We're all in. It's over, boys. We lay down our weapons and take what we can get. Only a damn fool keeps battering on and on at the same thing that's got them nowhere for donkey's.

'So the word is, a permanent cessation of operations, and put everything we have into building a mass movement on the ground. Wait to outbreed them, and then push for a referendum. But for the military side, the physical-force strategy, we wave the white flag. Accept decommissioning, and call off the armed campaign, once and for all. That's the word from the very top. It's over, boys.'

Nothing for a minute. You could hear their thick heads ticking, chewing it over.

And then.

Well, if you'd heard the whoops. The cheers and yo-hos. 'Let's get to fuck out of this. I knew the whole thing was a bad job this long time.' Coats on and downstairs to the bar. Barged right past Pig and Sid. The booze bruck out. Open tab for the whole place. Young lads shaking bottles of Buckie like Formula One. Like as if it was the Brits had announced a surrender, not the other way round.

Pig shook his head when Sid wanted to hammer some

sense in. 'Give them a wee minute to think it through. I know these boys. Before the evening's out they'll be begging us to keep the struggle going.'

Word went round the townland like wildfire, a mega session on at the Ships. In half an hour, every wannabee and hanger-on and balloon was there, jumping up and down to Bryan Adams Summer of '69 like a culchie wedding. Even some of the squad got dragged along, caught up in the fun. It spilled out in the street, can-cans and congas, Rock the Boat in the middle of the road, everybody dooting their horns as they drove by. Big smiles and wide wide eyes. Like weans in the tuck shop. You could see where it was leading. Dumps opened, balaclavas burned. Peace prizes handed out. Handshakes at the White House. Good suits and stripy ties and fat salaries at Stormont.

Phone calls were flying around, asking was it true. Belfast was on the blower, chewing the ear off Sid. 'Get a lid on it, fast, before this spreads round the whole of the North, for the Big Boy's doing his nut here. You're throwing away the only edge we have. If word gets out, somebody's got some serious explaining to do. There's more at stake in these talks than you know.'

So Sid went out and around. Cleaning up Pig's mess, as per usual. A quiet wee word with the rest of the squad. 'The boss man is up to something, this is just him testing the lads. Keep them in line, will you? We look very bad if word of this gets out.'

But he knocked the heads of the young ones. 'Were you ordered out in the streets? Who's running this show, us or youse? Get back in line. There's only one OC and you do what he says, or your knees'll know about it.'

And they all calmed the heads, did what they were bid, got themselves in order and quietened down. All except one man alone, a dirty wee carn known as Thirsty. Never had a penny to his name, but he could put it away like no other. Got free pints in the Ships for collecting up empties, and he'd finish every half-drunk glass in the place. The ugliest lumpiest fucker in the townland. Bow-legged, one lame foot, bony shoulders and a pointy baldy head with hair round the ears like a mangy rat. And here he was now, stumbling about the street, slurring at Pig, scoffing and scorning, all he was good for. At the same time, he was speaking for plenty who didn't dare open their bakes.

'Do you know what I say, boys? Let's turn in this fucking Pig to be stuck by the fucking Brits and take home the fucking cash. He's lucky Achill didn't put a bullet in his fucking brain already, that's all I can say. The same boy has done too fucking well out of this here war. Do you see the fucking motors he has beyond? If you knew what he has stashed away in the fucking Channel Islands, the fucking women he has coming and going. And that's what we're fucking fighting for! Him and his fucking women! Dog has the woman leave him, Pig takes Achill's woman, and we have to sort out their dirty fucking washing, run around dodging the Brits, ferrying guns, mixing squibs, touting on touts, ducking choppers, getting our houses tore to bits, our women felt up, our children tormented. For what? What fucking good has any of it done any of us? There's been no fucking state oppression here this twenty years. Who the fuck cares who pays your wages and your dole? Does any of you seriously think you'd be better off with that fucking shower in the South running the show? Crooked, thick, useless, desperate to suck up to hard cash and line their own fucking pockets. And here's London spraying their own pound notes at us like shite from a fucking muck-spreader, and youse all want to clear them out? A bit of fucking sense. Let's be rid of these fucking hoods once and for all so we can stop looking over our shoulders every day to see if our own fucking side is coming at us with a knife in the fucking back. If you ask me, I'll take the fucking Brits over the fucking Ra any day of the fucking week.'

That was enough for Sid. He lifted wee Thirsty by the collar and dragged him round the back of the Ships, the yard where the kegs were stacked. A few hard men followed after.

'Was it not enough having your knees done for you last Christmas?' says Sid. 'And you still limping from it. I'm going to break my rule especially for you, and do them over again. Down on the ground quick, in that shuck, so the water cleans away the blood. This time I'm fixing you myself and I'm making sure they both get done right.'

He didn't need anybody to hold the boy down because the first sight of the AK and Thirsty was begging and babbling and doing exactly what he was told, to the letter.

But when the barrel came down, he balled himself up, knees to his cheeks. Couldn't help it. So Sid pressed the wee end of it against his nose, pushed it hard on the bone between his eyes.

'Lie down there flat, or it'll be your wrists and your ankles as well.'

And he did, still weeping and whining.

'Also, shut the fuck up.'

He did.

The lads were crowding in now to watch. A couple of them helped out with the needful. Big thick towels around both legs, for the mess, and to muffle the noise. The end of the barrel dug in snug.

Pop. And pop. The both knees destroyed. Done right this time. Then a tin of emulsion poured on the fresh wounds, to slow up the surgery. The stupid prick wouldn't forget this one in a hurry.

The crowd gathered around all gave Sid a round of applause, a few slaps on the back, a lot of sniggering at Thirsty's shrieking and yodelling.

'Fair play to you. That'll shut him up another while. You have to hand it to Sid, he always knows the right thing to do, and that was the best show we seen this long time. It'll be a while before there's any more slagging the OC or talking about surrender in this here townland.'

Sid rounded on them all.

'You're a disgrace, the lot of you. There's not one of you any better than that cunt, and plenty worse, for at least he has the guts to say it to my face. Every one of you bogmen votes for a united Ireland, sings the songs, prays for it, marches for it, but when it comes to actually lifting a finger when there's real work to get done, you're all cheering a surrender? Well I'm glad the OC tested your stuff, for I'm ashamed of you all this day. We were told, our fathers were told, in 1969, that this work would take a generation, and that's exactly what it's taken. A good quarter of a century, and we're almost there. We've worn them right down to the threads, and now you want to pack up and hand them a victory they don't deserve, because somebody might break a fingernail? Pack of women!'

In the car and away. Left them standing there shuffling and muttering, mugs on them like a wet bank holiday.

8

Inside in the Ships, old Ned was waiting. He'd seen it all before. He had the men pull down the shutters, and he sat them all down again in the lounge, fresh pints on the house. The words came flying out of him.

'Now, lookit. Nobody likes a chewing. But thon Sid has brains to burn, and he wouldn't waste his breath if he didn't know youse all had the stuff for the fight, every last one of you. And it's a fight we're going to win. Wait now till I tell you how I know.

'They can throw everything at us, like they did at Mahatma Gandhi, like they did at Fidel Castro, like they did at Martin Luther King and Nelson frigging Mandela. But history only goes one way. And that way is to freedom. It might not be this week, nor this year, but that day is coming, and let me tell you this. All the names of them who fought for that freedom will be honoured on that day. No exceptions. And let me tell you what else. The ones who turned their backs when the going got tough will get spat at in the streets.

'You all know the cry that's been heard down the generations. *Tiocfaidh ár lá!* Our day will come! And that's as sure as the sun's going to rise in the morning. For we don't say might come, nor should come, nor ought to come. Will come! Let it take another year, or another hundred. You, or your children, or your children's children, are going to wake up one fine morning in a free and democratic thirty-two-county republic. But every day we fling away gabbing and squabbling adds another day to the wait. What do you say, Pig? Remind this townland of the stock they spring from, and that'll get the blood up rightly.'

'Good man yourself, Ned,' says Pig. 'That's the stuff to give them. If we had a dozen more like you, we'd have the Brits out tomorrow. Instead, look at the state of me, fighting over a woman. If you could only get myself and Achill ploughing the same field, this land would be free in no time.

'But you all heard the man. We need no slacking now. Freedom is coming, but it's not coming out the barracks gate on a silver platter. We have to batter that gate in and take it.

'So make sure you have a full tank in your car in case it's needed on the night, and make sure the key is left in your front and your back door both, in case a volunteer on the run might have to pass through. Keep your ear to the ground, and you'll be called on when you're needed. There'll be no let-up until this job is done, and done right.'

That set them straight.

9

I'd be all day naming every man in the townland who was behind that squad, their fathers and grandfathers, their wives and sons and daughters, and who married who. Enough to tell you about the big men, who sat in the Ships that night.

Pig himself, born and reared in the place, and his father once owned half the land. The da made his money from smuggling and he bought up all the neighbour farms with a bit of persuasion, then sold them back over the years at twice the price, and put it all into the cause. His brother Dog, a dacenter man but just as proud. Cross either of them, and you'd be in the hospital first and asked questions later. Their mother was Kelly from across the border, the townland of Tullybane, and she carried the fortune with her that set their da on his feet.

Then there was Sid, the smartest of the bunch. Vincent Little was the name he was called, the son of Tom Little had the pub at the crossroads that was burned out in the seventies, and the family moved to England. Wee Vinnie was sent back to be raised by his uncle Sean, a solicitor, for the boy was getting nowhere over beyond. He was always at the books, anything he could get hold of. Talk you into thinking black was white, they used to say. When the uncle died, the story was he left a fair whack to Sid, and right enough he never seemed to have much in the way of a job. But he was always around, helping people out, arguing their case, getting them their rights. No flies on Sid.

From the townland of Killymack, Jack Hughes, known to some as Zola, and to the rest of them as Budd, from the wee South African runner. The mightiest lump of a man that ever fought for the Ra. Near seven foot, and built like Finn McCool. No peeler would give him hassle, for fear of a busted nose he didn't even mean to give you. At school he'd been landed with the nickname Zola, when the teacher was teaching them about the Jews and the Nazis, and he started off with the Dreyfus Affair, about the Jew in the French army accused of touting to the Germans, who got stitched up by his own side. And the boys were made read a thing by this writer called Zola, and the thing was called *J'Accuse*. And once the boys heard that, Jack Hughes was called nothing but Zola from that day on. Or, until Zola Budd was back on the news, and then it got changed to Budd.

From Glencross, Dermot Slevin, known as Jack because he worked under cars, but in the squad he was always called the Other Jack, because of Budd. His da, Buck Slevin, had the wee video shop at the foot of the town, and a shelf of pornos under the counter if you knew how to ask. The mother was Kitty Doyle from Newry, with the sister was the baby nurse and the brother the dole man everybody juked.

The whole squad went back to Pig's place, and a fry was

put on the pan, good thick pink-and-white rashers, skinny sausages still in a string, rough-cut slices of purple black pudding, eggs spitting and crackling, the rim crisping up gold and then brown and then black. And all slid onto plates and shared among the men. The tea poured out, hot from the pot, the milk in a jug and sugar spooned in. That's more like it. Plates clean, fags out, and a bit of quiet oul chat.

They started planning the recce. In the car, scope out the best spot for the squib, where to keep an eye, who was doing what. Each of them had his wee job to do, and each got on with it. Dry runs, measuring out, noting the times of patrols, buying the bits and pieces they'd need from enough different shops that they'd never be traced.

Back in business. Things were looking up.

Nellie

10

You could argue the bit back and forth which was the very moment, right from the Easter Sunday when she was hatched out of the egg, like her da used to say, all the way up to the first time she met you-know-who. But I'd say the right place to start is slap bang in the middle of things, back about three years before, when Nellie was a schoolgirl of sixteen.

She had a wee thing going with a lad from her big brother's class. Brian Campbell was the name. The star of the hurley team. A tough nut on the pitch. A real swagger about him round the townland. Never said much. You felt ten foot tall if he nodded you hello going past. Even your ma and da would nudge other and point him out.

She'd had a few sniffing round her. Everybody said she was the best-looking in her year. Maybe in the whole school. She didn't like closing off her options, so she kept stringing them along. You'd see her up the town, marching about with three or four fellas trailing after.

In the end, Brian's mate Sid took her aside and said to make up her mind before there was a real barney between some of them. Told her if she couldn't decide, to just give each of them a number and roll a dice. That was what he did himself when there were too many options to toss a coin. He said you didn't have to do what the dice said, but how you felt when the number came up would show you what you really wanted.

Brian's number came up. She was fucking delighted.

She wore the face off him at the Glenallen the next Saturday, and that was that. Sid put the word out that nobody was to kick up. Not that they would have, to Brian.

11

Brian wasn't really into drinking, or music, or cars, like the rest of them. Beagles was his thing. He was always out hunting, when he wasn't at hurley practice. He said he knew every inch of the country around. Nellie asked if she could go along with him. It was a wee test. She was pretty sure he had another girl on the go as well, but he never said, and she never asked. Playing the long game.

He said okay. That was what she wanted to hear.

She used to tell her ma and da she was going to her friend Laura's house, from the drama group, but Brian would pick her up round the corner. They'd go for a drive up the hills. There was a wee outhouse he was let use, to keep his hunting stuff. A wee mattress in it. They'd have a wee cuddle. They'd have a wee snog.

That was as far as it went. She wouldn't give him the ride. Not yet. Nor she wouldn't let him finger her. She wouldn't even pull him off. She was still a virgin, do you see. Everybody in her class was, or they said they were, though to listen to the lads, you'd wonder who was lying. To be fair to Brian, he never pushed it. She liked that about him.

This one day he was sitting round the back of the outhouse smoking a jay. He didn't like doing it inside in case his brother smelt it. His brother would murder him if he caught him, he told her. She didn't go out and join him, because it was cold, and she didn't want any. She was happy enough, for once, just sitting there, waiting on him to finish.

But she was getting cold now herself. She put on a jacket that was hanging up on a peg. She could feel some tools or something heavy clattering in the pocket. She took them out.

It was two guns.

She thought she was going to faint. She thought she was going to boke. She said 'Oh fuck' and he heard her and came in. He said 'Oh fuck' too.

She held them out to him like a question. She needed to know.

He told her the coat was his big brother Shane's. He used the outhouse as well. Brian swore blind that he didn't know the guns were there.

She asked if his brother was in the IRA. Brian said he didn't know, but he thought he probably was. He hung around with that crowd.

Brian said she'd better put them back, and say nothing. She did. He said to take them out again, and wipe them down in case her fingerprints were on them now. She said she didn't know how. He did it for her.

She watched him, and she could see plain he'd done it before.

And then she knew, as sure as if he'd told her, that the coat was his, and the guns were his.

But she knew not to say. She knew never to say.

He asked her if she wanted to lie down. He said he was

feeling stressed now. She had made him stressed and he needed to lie down. She said she was feeling stressed too, and she needed to lie down as well. So they did.

It was true. She was feeling very fucking stressed. She didn't know what to think. She'd honestly never thought too much about all that shite. It was just there, like the weather. She wasn't against it. But she'd never been mixed up in it before. She'd never wanted to be.

Except she knew she still wanted him. Big time.

And this was it, she decided. Stick or twist. She could have him right now this minute, or let him get away. She tossed the coin in her head, and it came up with her letting him get away.

No fucking way. She was having him right now.

Straight out she asked him if he wanted a handjob. She said it would calm him down. She said she knew he always did it himself anyway after they'd had a cuddle, when she was dozing, and she didn't mind. She said she sometimes did herself as well, when he was snoozing, so there was no point hiding it. He said, 'Fuck it, sure why not.'

She asked him if he would start himself off. He said no way, if she was watching. He'd be too self-conscious. She told him to close his eyes and she would too.

She didn't. She watched his face. She was imagining how it felt. Then she took it in her hand, and tried to copy what he was doing. She loved seeing the look on his face when she got the rhythm right.

He stopped her, and said, 'Look, I don't want to count my chickens, but just so you know, I have no johnnies.'

'I have one in my bag,' she said. 'But that's where it's staying. Just so you know.'

When she reckoned he was ready to pop, she put her lips over the end, like she'd seen in a porno one time. She kept on pulling, but tried to move her head as well. When he came, she near choked. It slipped out, and then she was covered in the stuff. He said, 'Don't stop now, for Jesus sake!' And he grabbed it himself and gave another few tugs, till he was all done. She was up on her feet, shaking the gunk off her hands, and wiping it off her face. It was fucking disgusting.

'That was fucking disgusting,' she said. 'I tell you right now, Brian Campbell, I am never doing that again. You are one dirty scut.'

He was panting like a dog.

'Calm down, would you. I never asked you to in the first place. Frig sake.'

She got some tissues, and the two of them cleaned themselves up.

Neither of them said anything for a few minutes. She didn't know what to do now. She felt stupid. She hoped she hadn't ruined it. Her and her smart fucking mouth.

'Well, the first time's always the most romantic, so they say.'

He said nothing. She could feel him slipping away. Only one thing for it.

'We can have another go in a minute, sure.'

'I thought you said you were never doing that again.'

'Neither I am. Grab us up my bag, till I find that johnny.'

12

After that, the pair of them were inseparable. He met Nellie every evening after school. She went down to watch him at hurley practice. She went out hunting with him really. You'd see them sitting in Franco's Cafe after school, grinning at other, bantering away. Her ma and da didn't mind one bit. They thought Brian was a lovely fella. And the family was very well off. Fingers in lots of pies. The pumps at the border, loads of livestock, plenty of property in the town. Sponsored the youth club, and paid for the coaches to Medjugorje every year. Always happy to sort out a wee matter for you if you had a word. You'd hear the odd rumour about smuggling, but nobody minded that. Not a bit of it.

The odd time you'd hear people muttering about the da, and what he was mixed up in. She'd heard a man say that Brian's father was one lad you wouldn't want to cross. That there was more than livestock being smuggled over the border. You never saw him in pubs or down the town. He seemed to get stopped by the soldiers an awful lot, but so did plenty of people. That proved nothing.

She was there with Brian the day his da had a heart attack after Mass. The priest had preached about how you couldn't come to the chapel and take communion if you were in any way supporting the IRA. A few standing in the porch at the back decided to leave. The priest said he noticed them leaving, and that was fine, anybody whose conscience wasn't clear was perfectly correct to go on home, and they were welcome back when they were at peace with themselves, and with their Lord, and with their community.

Nellie still didn't think very much about all that. Brian never talked about it, so neither did she. But everybody she knew supported a united Ireland. The majority of the area would have nothing to do with Sinn Fein or the IRA, solid respectable SDLP voters, but you still knew that they were sound. Going about the right thing in the wrong way, is what both lots would say about the other. Even if you hated the Provos, and there were some who had good reason, you never took the side of the Brits. Ordinary Protestants getting shot or blew up was a different thing. Nobody liked hearing that. But soldiers were soldiers and they knew what they were getting into. You might feel a bit sorry for them, as individuals, or for their families, but it was completely fair enough at the same time. In for a penny.

So whenever everybody was leaving that day, all the talk was about what the priest said. Whether he might find his milk bottles broke in the morning, or his tyres slashed, or his windows in.

Out in the car park there was a bit of a kerfuffle. Brian's da was on the ground. A few men laughed. They thought he was playacting, pretending to faint with the shock. But then he wasn't moving. The men were calling for a doctor. There was a nurse getting in her car, and she got out again and ran over. Brian shouted had anybody got a mobile phone and could they call an ambulance. Somebody did. The nurse kept his head up with her handbag and worked at his heart. Francie Donnelly raced up to the hotel to get Dr Mallon, for Olive Farrell said she'd seen him going in for his dinner. The ambulance came, and Brian's da was taken up to Craigavon. The boys followed in the car. He was dead before they got there.

Later on a rumour went round that one of the paramedics was the brother of a man shot by the IRA years before, and he'd switched off the machine on the way. The boys didn't pay any heed. You always got stories like that. You'd go mad if you listened to them.

It was the biggest funeral in many's the year. People came from all over. England, Scotland, America, Australia. The two boys were there for an hour shaking hands by the grave. The rain came on but they wouldn't budge. Nodding and muttering thanks and taking all the slaps on the back. A few serious-looking whispers in the ear from certain individuals. They were pale but there wasn't a tear. Though with the rain, it was awful hard to tell.

Their uncle got the property, but Brian's big brother Shane got the farm and the pumps both. He was five years older, and he was already working there. He knew the ropes. Brian dropped out of school and started working with him. It was what he would have done anyway in a few years. Everybody said it was the right thing. There needed to be the two of them, because the way the business was going, there'd be more and more trips away, and somebody had to hold the fort. There was the pigs at home, and the sheep out at Lanecross, and the old Cunningham farm they rented on and off for storage, to keep the tools and the plant, and whatever else. You know yourself.

Brian started spending less time with Nellie. He said he was always busy. She said that was fair enough. She was getting fed up with him anyway. He'd started acting weird since his da died. He hardly ever laughed any more. He was always with his brother, and three or four other ones, that she knew didn't like her being around. She wasn't thick. She knew the score.

She said maybe it was time they left it be. He said whatever suited herself. She said fine. And that was the end of it.

Indeed and it was not. He'd be back. She knew how to reel him in. The long game.

13

Nellie started hanging around with a few of the goths and the indie kids. Reading *Hot Press* and the *NME*, and watching *Network 7*. Listening to different music. She went up Belfast every month just to buy *The Face*, and see what she could pick up in Fresh Garbage or the market.

For a while, she had a wee thing going with Aidy McCann. He played in a thrash band with his brother Davy. Then she swapped him for Davy. The two lads stopped talking to each other for a while. The band kept going, though. They had a lot of bookings.

Then she started going out with Jarlath Mallon, the doctor's son. You couldn't miss him. He dyed his hair black, wore army trousers, and smoked rollups. He started taking her to Belfast, to student nights at the art college. He was very into his drugs, and she tried whatever was going. He knew some quare characters. One time they ended up at this rave in the middle of a field. Another time they climbed to the top of Cave Hill and lit a fire with these men with straw heads. There was some mad stuff going on.

At the same time, things were changing at the Glenallen. It was round the time everybody started doing E. You took a couple of them, and you just felt like all the worry and

stress and headfuck melted away. There was nothing but
the beat of the music

bom-cha bom-cha bom-cha bom-cha

the lights zooming all round you

your blood smiling up and down your veins

bom-cha bom-cha bom-cha bom-cha

you knew the best thing the only thing was to be close
to someone anyone that person right there and you knew
they felt the same

it was raining love

not the way it was with your family real love happy love

bom-cha bom-cha bom-cha bom-cha

love love love look there it goes whoosh up in the air
and whee down again

love love everywhere

and they all felt the same. She'd never felt closer to
anybody in her life.

Brian didn't seem bothered, when she saw him around.
But she wasn't that bothered herself any more. These were
her people now. They talked all kinds of stuff she'd never
thought about. Some of them said they didn't believe in
God. One fella said he thought he was gay. A few of them
were even Protestants. They were all for going to college,
maybe over in Scotland or Liverpool. A couple of them
talked about heading for London after, and not just to make
a few pounds. They were for staying. Getting the fuck out
this place. For good.

She'd honestly never thought about that before.

She thought about it now.

Finding yourself. Being yourself. Whoever you wanted to be.

She wondered what Brian would think. And then she realised she didn't give a fuck any more. He could follow her if he wanted. And if he didn't, his loss.

She knew she was good looking, but she always just went with the flow, wearing what everybody was wearing. Now she wanted to cut her hair short. Sinead O'Connor short. Her ma would hate it, but her da always said he thought it looked well.

She'd pierce her nose. Nobody she knew had done that. She was thinking about a tattoo, even. Maybe that was too much. She would wait till she got well away, and then she could do whatever she wanted. Whatever the fuck she wanted.

Could she really?

She really could.

Every day felt like a prison sentence. She wanted to scream. She knew there was another kind of life waiting for her. She could feel it. She didn't know the shape of it, or the ends of it, but she knew there was something inside her that could grow into anything at all, if she had the room. It was like the walls needed to be moved back. Now she knew there was an outside, the inside felt tiny.

She'd save up. She'd go to the tech, get her A-levels, and away to university in England. That was all she thought about. Nothing else mattered. She didn't give a fuck. She felt ruthless. The minute she knew she could do it, she knew she couldn't not. There wasn't a thing in the world would stop her. She'd do whatever it took.

But she wasn't going to fuck it up by telling anybody. The sneering and the slagging and the bitching. No way. Not even Jarlath. She'd wait on her chance. That was one thing she did know how to do. The long game. And when she saw that chance, no matter what it was, you wouldn't see her for dust.

14

Then she missed her period.

She knew straight away. It was always totally regular. And she felt different, inside. She could sense it, in her blood. She just knew.

And she knew what she had to do. Not a doubt for one second. All she needed was money. Money to get over to England and get sorted out. Mortal sin or not.

But she didn't know how. Not a baldy notion. She was panicking inside, but she just kept going about her business like everything was fine. Pretending it wasn't happening.

Her parents never knew a thing. Neither did Jarlath. They'd only really screwed three or four times, but always on E, and she couldn't swear he'd worn a johnny every time. The fucking stupid dick.

15

She wised up. She knew she had to do something, and fast.

Her friend Laura had told her one time that a teacher at her school was made leave because she got pregnant and she wasn't married, but what happened in the end was, she went to England to get rid of it, and then she was allowed keep her job. Laura said she knew all about it because her da had helped organise it.

Laura was a Protestant, and her da was a peeler. Nellie was the first Catholic her own age she ever spoke to, and she had made Nellie swear not to tell anybody round where she lived what his job was. Nellie couldn't care less, but she didn't mind Laura asking. She got the picture.

So Nellie told Laura her secret. She didn't know what else to do.

Laura was all biz. She said she could find out from her da how it worked. Nellie said no way. Laura said not to worry. She'd say she needed to know for a school project, or a story she was writing. Something. Her da was sound as a pound. Everything would be grand.

16

Laura's da picked the two girls up after drama group next time, and he said Nellie was to come back for her tea. She couldn't believe they had a bottle of wine on the table while they were eating. Not that they opened it.

After, she said she'd ring her brother for a lift, but Laura's da wouldn't hear of it.

'I'll drop you home. Not a bother.'

A bit of chat on the way, the usual nothing. He pulled up round the corner from her house, and turned off the engine.

'Now, listen. Before you go in home. I understand you might be in a wee bit of trouble. Is that right?'

Nellie was raging. Laura, the stupid fucking bitch.

'Don't blame my daughter. I guessed the whole story before she said a word. In the police you learn how to pick these things up.'

Nellie just looked at him. Say nothing, Brian always used to tell her. Let them do all the talking.

'Now, listen. I'm not a Bible-basher myself. I know you're a kind girl, a good girl. Things happen, and that's all right. You can go to England, and that's one way. But it costs money, and it takes a good few days. Not easy to sort out, at your age, never mind keeping it hush-hush. Which I'm assuming is what you want.

'Or there is another way. You see, I know people who could organise you to have the thing dealt with over here, very simple and very quick. Done properly, a real doctor. You'd only be away a half a day. We tell your parents it's a school project, or a drama-group trip, or something like that. I'll take care of that end of things, don't you worry. What do you say?'

'Does that not cost money?'

'Not as such, no. All you'd owe me is a wee favour. I'd need a bit of a hand from you now and again, but I can see you're a good girl. A kind girl. You don't want anything bad to happen to anybody. Isn't that right?'

'What kind of a hand?'

He lit a fag, a Benson, and offered her one too. She knew rightly what he was at. Trying to make a wee secret to have between them. Show her he thought she was grown up enough. See if she said no, and that might mean she wanted to keep it. Cheap tricks. But a fag was a fag, so she took it.

'Ah, nothing much at all. Just the very odd wee bit of information. For example, I might show you a picture, and say do you know that man's name. Or if you hear some oul chat on the bus, or at school, or out at the disco, you might let me know. I believe you've some history with a certain individual who would be up to no good now and again, and we just want to keep that sort of character on a short lead. Do you get me?'

'You want me to tout?'

'Not at all, no such thing. Goodness gracious, no. We

have enough of those people, and they do what they do. I just mean confirming things we already know, more or less. Adding a wee piece to the puzzle. Touts, as you call them, are individuals who are actively involved, but they're really working for us, or for the army. Agents, we call them. Making things happen on the inside. That's a very different matter, and it's important, but it's highly specialised work. This here I'm talking about is wee buns. Just helping us see what's going on. Like wiping somebody's glasses for them. There's far more people passing on bits and pieces than you'd believe. Nobody will ever know a thing about it.'

'I think I should go in home now.'

'I understand, but just listen a wee second. This is the way it works. If there's to be an attack on a certain army foot patrol at a certain time, we just make sure that patrol doesn't go out. If there's to be a fuse or a timer taken from a dump that we can access, then we disable that timer and the device won't explode. The paramilitaries think it's faulty equipment, or bad luck, and nobody's the wiser. If we did any more than that, it might compromise the people who are helping us, and all we want to do is save lives. It's not gathering evidence, we're not going to arrest anybody, or shoot anybody. The opposite. We're only interested in saving lives. Do you see what I mean?'

'I really think I should go in now. They'll be wondering where I got to, so they will.'

She said nothing. Neither did he. She'd finished her fag, but she didn't know what to do with the butt, so she was just holding it, trying not to let the last bit of ash fall in his car. She could tell he knew rightly, and he was saying nothing on purpose, letting her feel uncomfortable. So they both just sat there.

Then he took it off her, and dropped it out the car window.

'That's okay. You don't have to do a thing you don't want to. Take your time, have a wee think. But not too long. The sooner you get the thing dealt with, the easier it'll be. And of course, if you get a better offer, good luck to you. Anyway, you know where to find me.'

17

It was an army doctor gave her the tablet, at a barracks in Lisburn. She had to sign a form first. Then she went back a few days later and took a different one as well. The doctor made her promise never to tell anybody, ever, or they might all go to jail.

It was pretty fucking grim while it was happening. But it didn't last long. And then it was over and done with.

The next few days, she felt very mixed up about the other side of it. She hadn't told anybody. Especially not Jarlath. She couldn't bring herself to go with him again, not now, so that was all finished with. She was on her own. But that was how she wanted to be. Who would have her now? She knew it was stupid, but she couldn't help feeling like everybody knew she was doing something shameful.

She phoned up Laura's da. There was nobody else. She said she was feeling very bad about the whole thing. It wasn't right.

'It's only natural to feel that. You did a hard thing, but it was a sensible thing. All part of growing up. There's more people round here than you'd believe who've done the same, Protestants and RCs both. Soldiers get themselves in bother sometimes, and it's always best to manage things on the QT. And every one of those people that I know of has fine children now, in a happy home and a happy marriage.'

'I don't mean that. I mean the other thing.'

'Oh, I see. Well, I mean, look. A debt is a debt, I'm afraid. There's no backing out at this stage. You scratch my back, and all that. But we're not asking you to do anything bad. And it might be something very good. It genuinely might save a life. I know you feel bad about the wee baby, so look at it this way. If you can save another life to balance it out, well and good.'

18

He said they'd make it a kind of routine. Every Wednesday after the drama group, she'd go back to their house for her tea, and then he'd leave her home, and they'd have a wee chat.

The first time she told him nothing. Just shite. Such-and-such was seen going into a well-known republican bar, when the dogs in the street knew the same boy was a diehard republican. She thought that would get her off the hook. But no. He said he could use his own two eyes. The men they were after would never be seen near a republican bar. He needed a bit more.

That put the wind up her. Big time. What the fuck was she playing at? This was serious shite she was getting mixed up in. She said she'd changed her mind. She would pay the money, whatever it was she owed, but she wasn't going to meet him again.

He told her he understood, but he was being transferred on to other duties, and so she would have to sort it out with his superior. He said to call in the station, tell people it was about getting her driving licence, and she could have a wee chat then.

The superior wasn't so nice. He shook his head, slow and steady, like a sarky teacher telling you you were getting detention.

'Changing your mind isn't on the cards, I'm afraid.'

'Can we not just forget about it? I won't say nothing, I swear to God.'

'What I propose is, we start paying you. Say, twenty quid a week? And I'll take over as your handler. Any time you have something for me, there's a few quid more. And if I get something I can actually use, then it's serious spondulicks.'

'I can't. It's not right.'

'That's a matter of perspective. But we're all sinners, aren't we? There's none of us has a stainless soul.'

'What's that supposed to mean?'

'I've had a look in your file, and I was quite taken aback at what I found. Pictures of you at the base in Lisburn that time. Copies of the form you signed, for the tablets. It's all there, chapter and verse. Oh, I'll not say anything, don't you worry. But word can get out different ways. It's just what you might call a wee insurance policy. You play ball, and so will we. Dead simple. Everybody's happy.'

19

She came up with a few bits and pieces. And they started giving her cash, far more than she expected. Sometimes fifty or a hundred pound. She got used to it very quick.

She always had what nobody else had. Clothes. Make-up. Hair. She was more beautiful all the time, they all said it. She could be a model. And she knew it was true. She wasn't interested in that kind of thing, but she was smart enough to know that if you looked a certain way, you had a head start in anything you wanted to do.

It wasn't vanity. It was good sense. There were few enough ways out of that place, and if an accident of birth had give her a wee leg up in one of them, she wasn't going to look a gift horse in the mouth. She'd take whatever she could get.

So she kept up her reports. And the cash kept coming in. This was her ticket out. Just a wee bit longer. Just another couple of hundred in the bank.

When the ceasefire was called, she thought that would scupper the whole thing. But her handler said quite the contrary. It was vital they knew what was going on inside the movement. It could break down at any time, and they needed some idea what was coming.

She got to hanging out with Brian's crowd again. Not

Michael Hughes

ones really involved, just young lads doing the odd message. But she thought it was safe enough now. She asked a few innocent questions, and she soon got a good idea who was who these days. It could change very fast.

She never saw Brian. People said he was over in England. Nobody ever said doing what. And damn sure nobody ever asked.

They started asking her to run the odd message herself. Her family was sound enough, but nothing to draw attention. She was a clean skin. She might come in handy herself some time. She okayed it with her handler, and that was that.

Before long she found herself drinking with some of the top men. They were never seen together in pubs, so it was always at somebody's house. She was let sit in the odd time. She could sing too, that helped. They liked having her around.

The peelers started dropping hints that she might try and click with one of them. Nothing mad, just the odd drink, maybe a wee snog and a fumble out the back of wherever. String him along, see what she could find out. She always said no, acted shocked, but they dangled big money in front of her. Hundreds, maybe thousands if they could secure a conviction.

Sometimes there'd be English fellas there when she met her handler. She could tell they weren't very popular with the RUC, always getting dirty looks. She got the feeling she was big news. Like the peelers and the army were fighting over her. She didn't mind that one bit.

Just another few months. Another five hundred quid. Soon she'd be set. Any day now.

20

Then Brian showed up.

She was working behind the bar in the pub right on the border where most of them drank. It was really called the Spanish Armada, but everybody called it the Ships, because of all the old pictures there were hanging on the walls. It had a few rooms upstairs so they could have a hotel licence, and keep the bar open as late as they liked. Some nights she would stay herself, to save waking them at home when she came in.

The job was her own idea. You heard everything, plus it gave her a cover story for the money. She was earning more every week from the peelers than she was in a month at the bar, but at home she used to say she got very good tips. Which was sometimes true. She knew how to. And it all added up. She gave a bit of money to her ma and da every month, and they never asked a thing. Her da had just been laid off again, and there was four younger than her at home. Money was money.

When she saw Brian that night, she got this plan in her head. It was just there. She could see it all laid out, like she was on top of a hill and it was the fields down below. She knew it was mad, but she also knew it was fucking brilliant. She'd tell him she was moving away, and it would only be a wee fling. If she could get something good out of him, and one big payout, that would be the truth.

No time like the present. And he was still a fucking ride.

Him and a couple more had been there for a while, watching the band, but now the place was shut and it was only them left. The other two were in the corner, full, singing rebel songs, and it was just Brian at the bar smoking fag after fag.

She joined him. They didn't look at each other, but she knew he knew she was there. She said it had been a while and he said it had indeed. She said he never used to smoke, not fags anyway, and he said aye well times have changed.

She asked him for one and he said to work away. She told him her hands were wet from wiping up and asked would he light it for her. She couldn't help it, she was feeling awful cheeky. She leaned in her head and he put it between her lips. She could taste just the slightest wee taste of him on the filter. The heart was thumping away in her chest.

He asked where the bogs were. She knew he knew rightly. She said the lights had gone in the toilets in the hall but there was an en suite room up above, and he could use the one in there. But he'd never find it on his own, the place was a rabbit warren, so she would have to show him. 'That's highly convenient,' he said. 'Isn't it just,' she said. And then she knew they were going to screw.

She was hot with excitement when she was undoing her bra. The face was flying off her, she could feel it. Doing the sums in her head while he started pawing at her. She'd worked out she needed five grand to get to England and get started, but every time she got anywhere near it, she dipped in. It was too hard not to get the bus up to Belfast and call in to Top Shop and get a few wee things. One big payout would put her over the top. This is it, she kept thinking. This is it.

They clicked again in that wee room. Just like old times. He clung onto her after like a limpet. Like one of them bears she used to have when she was wee. And he wouldn't let go.

He said they were getting married, and she said she was in no rush. He said he was, and just so she knew that's what was happening. She said nothing. It was the usual shite.

Except it wasn't. The next day down the town, everybody was coming up and congratulating her. He'd put it about the town that he came home to propose, and she'd said yes. Fuck. That wasn't the plan at all.

Her head was spinning. She had to nod and smile, and before she knew it, it was getting too late to say anything. Fuck fuck fuck.

There was no way out of it, not without a major scandal. And her ma and da were delighted. They needed a bit of good news. So she told herself it would be all right. Maybe it wasn't even the worst idea. Things were looking a bit different with the ceasefire. Sooner or later he'd be on the straight and narrow. Get him away from that whole crowd and making good clean money. Start working on him to move over to England.

So she went along with it. Because, what else do you do?

21

Nellie used to wonder did she love Brian. She wasn't too sure how she was supposed to know. Which meant the answer was probably no. He never said it in so many words, so she didn't either.

But she had the feeling he was the sappier of the pair of them. He was the one who would get all lovey-dovey when he had drink taken. You're everything to me. I would die if you left me. I would kill any man who laid a finger on you. I would track him down, and I would take off the side of his house with a JCB, and I would nail him to the fucking wall.

She could tell he thought this kind of shite was romantic, but she also knew he kind of meant it. Men were such dicks. Some days she used to hate that you had to bother with them at all. There weren't three decent ones in the whole place.

She told her handler they were together, and that meant she was finished. He got het up, and said there might need to be changes. She was asked to come into the barracks one day, a different barracks, and one of the old hands asked her how she'd feel about working for the army instead of the police. It would be bigger money but they would need a better class of information. She said no fucking way.

She was done. He said these were very special circumstances, and she could name her price. She told him she appreciated the offer, but she was hanging up her spurs. It wasn't worth it.

He didn't like that. He said they might have to turn her in to the Ra. Or do some graffiti saying she was sucking off peelers. Or get her wee brother kneecapped. The thing was, she was to stay put. That was all there was to it. She was an agent. She didn't get to pick and choose. She had a duty. They wouldn't leave her high and dry, but they wouldn't let her dictate terms either. She didn't have a choice in the matter.

22

It all happened very fucking fast. She was only just eighteen. But everybody was dead excited, and she was too. She couldn't help it.

It was nothing over the top, but he did it right. Everybody said it was a lovely day.

The shine went off it very fast, but. He took her for a week in Donegal after, by way of a honeymoon. Most of it she spent sitting on her hole staring out at the rain while he went and caught up with various old friends in the area, and came stumbling back in at three in the morning. She knew rightly what he was up to, but he said nothing. Neither did she. But she was already starting to wonder if she'd made the worst fucking mistake of her life.

23

When she got back, she was assigned a new handler, an army fella. She was to meet him every week in a different base, a good way away. She told Brian she was doing a hairdressing course. She knew he couldn't give a fuck.

The handler said his name was Alex. Proper stuck-up English accent. Except he wasn't at all. He was good crack, in his own way.

She heard one of the other soldiers slagging him, calling him Paris. She asked him why. He said it was because when he first started, he overdid the amusing anecdotes about his time at the British Embassy over there. They said every time he opened his mouth, it was 'When I was in Paris'. He thought they were exaggerating, but once something sticks in the army, that's it. They were always leaving berets and strings of onions on his desk.

And he was a ride and a half. Oh my God. She could have jumped his bones right there and then. She watched his eyes watching her, and she knew he felt the same.

He was hers. There was no way he wasn't.

All the lights went on inside her head. She was up on the top of that hill again, but the landscape was a different one now. The only question was, did she have the nerve?

Fucking right she did. Double or quits.

24

She did nothing for a couple of months. It was all fairly quiet anyway, and there was nothing much to tell them. Then she started acting worried, and asking Alex what happened if Brian got on to her.

He explained about giving her a new identity. That would only happen if she was compromised, he said, and if he recommended they take that particular course of action. He said it was extremely unlikely they would agree even so, and so really not worth thinking about. She said she knew that, but it would settle her head just to know how it would all work in theory.

He explained she would be set up with a house or a flat in England, with rent paid for six months, and a job, and a new name. After six months, she'd have to fend for herself financially, but they would keep an eye on her, and if she thought she was in real trouble there were ways they could help. At home, it would be as if she just disappeared. If they had to, they could fake her death, but usually it was pretty obvious to people what had happened. She would just have to live with that. She'd have to wipe the slate clean, start a completely new life as a completely new person.

That was what she was waiting to hear.

She let things run along another wee while. She started

playing it up, to put him off the scent. Saying all the time how certain she was she was doing the right thing, how she was so happy to have this opportunity to help bring the violence to an end once and for all.

Then she started saying she thought Brian was getting suspicious. That he kept telling her they had an idea there was a tout in the unit, and dropping big hints. That a couple of times he'd got drunk and beaten her up. She showed him bruises. They weren't real. She did them herself with make-up. Well, most of them. Some of them were from screwing.

None of it was true. Brian never laid a finger on her. She hardly saw him at all these days, except when he turned up half-cut and wanted his hole. Then it started. She was on a pedestal to him. There was nothing she could do that he would stop loving her. Even if she was screwing another man, he would cut his balls off but he would still love her. He actually said one time that even if she was a tout, he would forgive her. He loved her that much.

She told Alex she'd heard Brian on the phone saying he was sure there was an informer very close to him personally, and they had a pretty good idea who it was, and they would be sorting that individual out the next week or two.

Alex didn't seem bothered at all. He told her they would monitor the situation. She could tell he knew rightly it was bullshit. She needed to get things moving, before that story was the truth.

Plan C.

25

She'd seen it on the TV, in *Grange Hill*. She wrote up a
kind of a diary. Her and Alex. What she'd want it to be
like, if they got together. Teenage stuff, she knew it, but
it was good crack to write. She left it behind one day,
accidentally-on-purpose, so she was sure he had read it. He
never said when he handed it back, but she could tell he
was different after that.

He came in one day and said he'd found a flat for her
in Birmingham. It wasn't lovely, he said. She could move
now, or wait for the next one to be free, but that might be
months or even years. She said she was up for it. He told
her to pack a bag, and make up a cover story that she was
away for a couple of weeks.

She'd had the bag packed for ages. She told Brian she
was away to visit her cousin in Liverpool who was splitting
up from her husband but couldn't tell anybody at home,
and she got the bus to Belfast. She wondered if he would
even miss her.

About halfway up the M1 she suddenly realised she would
probably never see him again. She couldn't keep the smile
off her face.

26

Alex met her at the bus station. He drove her to the ferry, and they crossed over to Scotland. He said it would be a hell of a run, but they couldn't risk flying, and they couldn't risk crossing the border to go by Wales. She snoozed in the car and he drove all day. It was about one in the morning when they got to the flat.

It was a one-bed basement shithole. It stank. There were mice, and God knows what else. It wasn't exactly what she'd had in mind. He said it was just until they could sort out something more suitable. She said it better be.

He said he'd be there too for the first few days, on the sofa, just to keep an eye. She said he didn't have to. He said in fact he did, those were his orders. She told him she meant on the sofa. He didn't have to. If he didn't want.

They sat looking at each other.

He said that would be very unprofessional. She said she wouldn't tell anybody if he didn't. It would just be to keep her company. She was feeling awful scared.

They sat looking at each other again.

She said it was up to him, and went in to bed. She must have fallen asleep, because next thing she felt the mattress sinking, and his big strong arms folding around her.

He was very gentle. Totally different than Brian. He took

his time. Kept asking her if it was okay. She told him she didn't want the football commentary, she just wanted to screw. But she liked it, kind of. And then him holding her after. God, that was nice.

27

She knew they'd be awful worried at home, so she took the risk and phoned her ma. She told her she'd met an English fella. He worked for the army, and she knew that was no good for the family, so she was moving over to England to be with him, and that was the end of it. Her ma roared and cried for a while, and then she wised up.

Her ma said she wouldn't lie, that Brian had been ringing up asking. It seemed he'd had some friends pay a wee visit to the cousin in Liverpool, and she knew nothing about it, said she hadn't seen Nellie in a couple of years. Which was true.

Nellie told her ma to say what she liked. She was finished with Brian, and she wasn't coming back. He might as well know the truth. Tell him she was another man's woman now, and there wasn't a damn thing he could do about it.

Talk about a red rag to a bull.

28

Alex came in one night with three other men. One of them was Special Branch, she'd met him before, one was army, because he said he was, and the one in a good suit and shiny shoes never said a word. Probably MI5, she reckoned. Or some other crowd she'd never heard tell of.

They told her they had information they'd like her to corroborate, and then they would see about moving her to a better place, and finding her a job. She said she'd need to know exactly what she was getting.

A flat with rent paid for six months was what they offered. She got them up to a year. A new identity. A decent job, and it had to be in London.

They agreed.

29

The next week, Alex told her it was going to happen. She was going to get a grilling from the big cheese, Lieutenant Colonel Bernard King. He was in charge of the area in question.

She was shitting herself. He said not to worry. Bernard was a decent sort. She'd be looked after. She wished he'd said that he would look after her. But he never.

On the day, Alex drove her to an army base. She would be taken in to see the old man, and he would show her some pictures, and she would identify the individuals.

He asked Nellie was she ready. She said she was.

Was she fuck.

She was sat on a plastic chair in a plywood hut, behind a trestle table, Alex beside her. He didn't look at her. She didn't want him to. The big cheese was sitting at the other side.

'Are they looking after you?'

'Yes, sir, thank you, sir.'

He gave her a wee smiley frown that said, You really don't need to call me sir. And she gave him a wee smiley frown back that said, Och I know, but sure old habits die hard after eight hundred years of oppression. Sir. And at least he had the good grace to blush, kind of, and look away, and have a wee cough to himself.

'Well,' he said. 'To business. I should introduce myself. Lieutenant Colonel Bernard King, and I'm taking personal charge of your debrief, at the request of the powers that be. You know why you're here, I take it. I'm going to show you some photographs, and I'll ask if you can identify the men in the pictures. Do you understand?'

'I do, aye.'

'These men are all watched closely. They're suspected to be the main players in the area. We've had intelligence that these players are up to no good. We suspect they're a threat to the current political situation, which has been very hard won, and we need them off the scene immediately. That's where you come in. All it takes is your word that they're members of PIRA, and then we can put them under surveillance, and when we have enough evidence, move to arrest them.'

'Members of what was that you said?'

'I beg your pardon?'

'Pyro, something like that.'

'PIRA. The Provisional IRA.'

'I never heard it called that before.'

He laid out the pictures on the desk. Mostly black and white, a few colour.

'Can you name these men?'

'Give me a wee minute.'

It freaked her out seeing them there. She knew every one of them.

'Let's start here. Do you know this man?'

'That's Ned Rice.'

'Is he a member of PIRA?'

'He is, aye.'

'Anything else you can tell us about him?'

'He's the old timer in the area. They keep him around out of respect, mostly, although he looks at the cars for them. He never shuts up once he starts. But he gives them a kind of kudos. And his son Anthony does wee jobs now and again.'

'Good. Thank you. This one?'

'Diamond McDaid.'

'Can you give us his real name?'

'Wait till I think. It might be Adrian. I'm not sure. Everybody calls him Diamond.'

'And is he a member of PIRA?'

'He is. And he's a fucking head-the-ball. Excuse me. You don't want to cross him. They used to say he'd go off and do his own operations sometimes. Nobody dared to say a thing, because he was a law unto himself. The only one he listened to was the boss man. They used to say if anything happened, Diamond was to take over, but I think they were all shit-scared of the idea. But the boss man liked him, so he kept him around.

'This one? Seamie Macken. Yes, he's a member of the IRA. He works as a vet, and he used to patch them up if they ever couldn't get to a doctor. His brother has the pumps near the border. They sometimes used his big shed out the back to make the mix. The last bomb in London was got ready there, I heard. They'd load it into bags, and hide them under hay in the back of a trailer. It would be kept over the border until it was needed. They'd take it over on the ferry, and drive it to where they needed it. That's what I heard, anyway.

'The curly haired one is Sid. He's a member of the IRA, do I have to keep saying it? These here in these pictures are all members of the IRA, so they are.'

'Thank you, but I'd be grateful if you would continue to identify them individually. Can you give me his real name?'

'Vincent Little, but they call him Sid Little after that eejit on the TV, because he wears glasses. I've known Sid for ages. He's the brains of the outfit. Could have been a priest or a teacher or anything. He was the one plotted and planned the jobs. Nothing would get past him. He's a lovely fella, but you wouldn't want to say the wrong thing either. A proper republican. He could talk the history at you all night. It was an education listening to him.

'This one's Jack Slevin, and he's a member of the IRA. Except he isn't really called Jack. He's Dermot, I think. He has a scar on his face where a car fell on him when the jack failed. And then about three months later the same thing happened again. He was lucky both times. So they always called him Jack, because it drove him fucking nuts. The boys loved getting a rise out of him. But then when he joined up with Budd, they started calling him the Other Jack, because Budd's name really is Jack.

'This one is Budd. Because of the wee runner with the bare feet, you know? Zola Budd. He was called Zola first, from school, I don't know why, probably something off the

TV, and then it got made into Zola Budd, and then just Budd. He's a fucking giant, and he's all muscle. Including between the ears, if you ask me.'

'And his real name?'

'Like I said, Jack. Or John Hughes, he was christened. And he's a member of the IRA.'

'Thank you. Now then. These two are the last.'

She was quiet for a minute.

'Is everything all right? Would you like a glass of water?'

'No, thanks. Sorry. That's Shane Campbell. He's a member of the IRA. He's the boss man, the OC in the area. He's known as Pig, because he farms pigs and smuggles them, and because he's very stubborn, some people say. And also, he's a fucking pig. But the whole family has that. The da was known as Horse, because he had a big long face, and he always kept horses. And the granda before him, he was called Bull, I think because he had a quare temper. And probably a bull as well, I don't know. Maybe he was always talking shite.'

'And this man?'

'His brother. Brian Campbell. Everybody calls him Dog.'

'And?'

'And what?'

'Is he a member of PIRA?'

She was looking at her nails. They needed done.

'I'm afraid we do need a positive identification in every case.'

'Fine. Yes.'

'Yes, he's a member of PIRA?'

'Fuck sake. Sorry. Yes he is. Is that it finished now?'

The big cheese gave her another one of his wee smiley frowns.

'We've barely started, my dear. Nothing you'd like to add, before we move on?'

She shrugged her shoulders.

'Let me be more direct. What is the nature of your relationship with Brian Campbell?'

'Fuck sake. Do we have to? You know rightly.'

'Even so, I'd be grateful if we could hear it first hand. Just for the record.'

'Fine, suit yourself. I'm his wife. Happy?'

Dog

30

The feelers were out, at the highest level. Letters were shuttling back and forth between London and Sinn Fein, with the usual suspects acting as go-betweens. There was a mountain to climb, for sure, but it wasn't going to happen until somebody got a pick in the ice.

Were they serious about wanting peace? Was either side? That was the question in the air at the talks. Can we still wind it down, if we're agreed on the destination? Dublin it was who let the cat out of the bag. If Sinn Fein and the IRA accept any deal that falls short of a united Ireland, then what the fuck had the last twenty-five years been for? Was it all a waste, the agony and the bloodshed these men had inflicted, never mind what they'd suffered themselves?

Now, any fool could see the answer was a big fat Yes, but there was no way they were selling that to the rank and file. Dublin tried to paint the picture. The one thing that had held the IRA together so far was the blind belief in armed struggle as the only viable means to achieve full thirty-two-county independence. Many of the higher-ups in the movement had long ago tumbled to the fact that all it had achieved was delaying the very thing they wanted to bring about, but admitting this would bring on a kind of madness. They couldn't even bring themselves to speak it.

They had to bull on regardless, and keep talking the talk, trying to turn the ship around so softly that nobody on board would notice a damn thing.

London asked the question, what have the British done that makes us worthy of this savage hate? A lot of nudging went on under the table, but nobody spoke. So it was smoothed over. But this issue can't afford to take over our agenda, was the next thing. There are far more important questions on which our two nations have to be united. On trade, on human rights, on the economy, on Europe. But there was a stern message for Dublin all the same. If we let you have your way on this, you've got to return the favour, and don't kick up a fuss when we disagree on some pet project of yours.

Dublin had no issue with that. No such thing at all at all, to be sure to be sure. They had no hint of a problem with any of it, they were just pointing out what would be acceptable to the republican movement itself. The stories we tell ourselves are just as important as the facts. And this side of the equation needed a story that they could spin into victory over the British, to prove to themselves that they hadn't surrendered, and they hadn't been wasting their time. Otherwise, nobody was dancing. That was all there was to it.

London took the point. Politics was politics.

They'd pass the word to the MOD. Keep it softly softly on the ground. Helmets swapped for berets. Fewer patrols, less hassle for the locals. Behind-the-scenes is the new upfront.

31

Barry Ross was smacked in the face by a cricket ball during basic training, and his eyes came up in two perfect black circles. So his brick started calling him Panda, because that's what he looked like. It stuck. He was glad. You had to be called something in this outfit, and he'd heard a whole lot worse.

The army was a bit like school, and Panda used to love school. The mucking about. Bending the rules. The banter. Constantly, constantly taking the piss. He didn't mind that it was mostly at his expense. He took it well, and that made him popular. He was let join in. He'd spent his whole life learning how to do it, and this was no different. Comparing shit tats in the showers. Sneaking a fag on duty. Chucking clingfilmed jobbies out of the chopper over the town. Having wee private ways of taking the piss out of the officers to their face, and they never knew. Except a few of them probably did. You had to feel sorry for some of those bastards. Not all of them, though. No way.

Sometimes it got to you, though. On patrol, trying to suss out every loner hanging around. Setting up a VCP, shining your torch on the licence, radioing through the details, waving them on. Keep it cold. Be civil, but never smile. Don't let your guard down. Any of them people could be trying to kill you. One or two of them would definitely love to. Most of them just wanted to get on with their day, right enough, but not a single one of them didn't wish you would go home and leave them the fuck alone. He knew they all hated him being there. So he tried his hardest to hate them back.

The IRA was getting inside his head. He could hear them, just daring him to come at them. He felt like a coward. He knew he was getting wobbly, and he was sure the rest of his brick could see it. Hard to know how to handle it. His CO was one of the touchy-feely types. Wanted to get him counselling.

Brass said it wasn't that bad. If every wobble gets a man home, they'll have no one left. These boys aren't dim. Everybody wants a way out, as long as they can save face. No one actually wants us here. Least of all us.

The messages started when he was out on patrol. He thought it was the radio first, but the rest of his brick never heard them. He said it must be his set was faulty.

But he figured it out pretty fast. It was coming direct to him. He'd had his wisdom teeth out during training, and he'd never felt the same since. Now he knew why.

They'd put a transmitter in his head, to get him messages direct from London. Sneer all you want, but he'd read about this sort of thing. It was well known. Documented. The Americans did it a lot. Special individuals they picked out for special missions. And his was to take out the enemy, single-handed.

That's right. Even up the score.

I'll be hung out to dry. A patsy like Oswald.

No. We'll take care of you. The cover-up is already arranged. You'll be a hero.

Panda felt sort of floating. Like everything was behind glass. That feeling of being in the back of the car when you're a kid, and the world is a wee bit muffled, and you're safe in your bubble.

Do you think it's right that he's walking the streets?

What can I do about it?

The same thing they do. Take on the enemy, any chance you get.

Panda felt like everybody knew. They were all staring at him. Whispering about him. He couldn't take much more of it. He was sinking. Going under. Weird fucking dreams waking him every couple of hours.

He'd have to go easy on the LSD. This new chef was doling it out. He was sure brass must be across it, but they didn't do a thing.

Jelly told him it was an experiment. The Americans did it in Vietnam. Specially modified acid, to increase aggression. Stig told them both it was nonsense. The brass were so naive they could take coke in front of them and they wouldn't know. Or care. They'd no idea what was going on in the real world.

These lads were coming in from towns where everybody was eating E like sweets. You could get it here as easily as there. Easier, for the paramilitaries sold it and protected the markets. There were whole multiples out that were totally mashed. Probably PIRA doing the same. Imagine that. Shooting at each other, both sides off their tits.

When he had leave, Panda drove around. He knew who. Watched the house. Waiting.

The third night, there he was. Brian Campbell. Panda could see him moving about behind the curtains. The bastard. He was going to come back some night and slot him.

Why come back?

Don't be thick. You can't just walk in and shoot.

They do it all the time.

But they're the bad guys.

You wouldn't think so, to watch the news.

And like he'd made a wish, the man stepped out of the house, into his car. Without stopping to think, Panda was after him.

This is it, he thought. I'm going to do it. I'm going to do it.

Attaboy. Do it. Do it now.

It was too easy. The man stopped in the wee car park by the library. Nobody else there. He stepped across into the bookies. Panda waited.

Out again, slip in hand. He sat in the car, poring over it.

This is it. I'm going to do it.

Yes you are. This is it. Do it.

I'm going to do it. This is it.

Panda drew the car up alongside. Kept it ticking over. Loaded his weapon down low, heart thumping. One round in, two, three, four. Another for luck.

Panda was ready to take his shot, like he knew that man

had done so many times. Just like he'd been told to. His special mission. He'd be a hero.

He raised the revolver. Gripped it tight in both hands. Squeezed the trigger.

Something exploded. His head. Fuck.

The car had lurched forwards, and he'd slammed back into the seat.

Some bastard rammed him from behind.

The target was off, burning rubber. Panda was out of the car.

'British Army!'

'IRA.'

He only saw the gun. Tried to duck. Too late. The bullet split the top of his nose between the eyes. It cracked his shiny teeth. The hard lead cut off his tongue at the root. It smashed his jaw. It gouged a ragged hole under his chin.

The black leaked down behind his eyes.

32

Pig nearly tumbled into the kitchen, and there was Dog on the floor, Pete Kearney by him, the table pushed away. His wee brother soaked in his own blood. It was leaking out of him, squeaking under Pig's gutties.

The big man was distraught. 'I promised our ma, when she was lying dying in this house here, in that wee room upstairs, that I would never let harm come to you. And now this is where I've led you! God forgive me.'

'Jesus, Pig. It's a flesh-wound. It's a fucking scratch.'

'Get Macken up here, now! I want my brother looked after, and that wound cleaned and dressed, or there'll be carnage this night. Is the bastard dead?'

Pete answered him, pacing around now like he was on the touchline.

'It was McDaid got him. Said it was clean through the nut. He was coming in to see Dog, about a horse. Only by chance he arrived the second your man was pulling the trigger.'

He lifted Dog out into the good room, stretched him on the sofa. Wee Brigid was waiting with cushions and blankets. Pig followed in, and back out again.

'Brit scum. Shoot-to-kill.'

'Jesus, Pig, that was no Brit. They don't just drive up in

plain clothes and empty you. It was the INLA, or some loyalist cunt.'

'Are you a child? Sure, half the shootings claimed by the splinter groups and the loyalists are done by undercover Brits.'

'Serious?'

'You pay too much heed to the news. Did you never think what the B in BBC stands for? And the R in RTE doesn't mean republican either, in case you were wondering. I tell you one thing, that's the end of the fucking cessation. We need to hit them back hard, and fast.'

'But sure, we can do nothing without Achill.'

Talk about the wrong thing to say. The kitchen table up on its end. Cups and dishes in bits on the floor.

'Fuck him! Do you hear me, Pete? I don't want to hear that name again!'

'Jesus sake, Pig.'

Sid heard the racket and stormed in, the Other Jack close after him.

'Just the men I want,' says Pig. 'Sid, put the word out. If they think we're laying down our weapons so they can lay into us, then they're getting the quare gunk, so they are. We're not that thick, bog Paddies and all that we are. Get the men roused up again. The job is on.'

'Pig, would you have sense. We've no mission, with Dog out of action too. They'll take us apart. And the higher-ups would disown us. We can do nothing without their say-so. We may just stay south till this one blows over. It might be months.'

'I'll give you blows over. Listen to me. Fuck the politicians. I say we're back on operations. We'll give it a couple of weeks to settle down, and then the minute we see an opening, we're ready to go. There's any number of men can step in for Dog. Domino, there's one. A dacent man, never touches a drop. Merrion's another. Sound him out. The two Jacks need nothing saying to them, we'll have to houl them back. Ned's champing at the bit, tuning up the motors. We run every plan by him, for he's seen it all. Sid and Pete, youse are for hanging back I suppose, looking after the ranch, while we go out and get stuck in. Fucking typical.'

'You're full of shit,' says Sid. 'Come over here and say that to my face.'

'Just you get on out there and do your job, and we can kiss and make up later on. You need fire in your belly, and I'm the boy to put it there. And get McDaid himself back on the scene. He's the hardest cunt I know.'

'He won't do it. He's out on his own this long time. Keeping the head down. Living out in Dallagh Forest in a tent, like Rambo.'

Pete was nodding away.

'It's true, Pig. Did you hear about thon oul fella got burned in his car there before Christmas? They say that was Diamond. The oul fella fiddled with his wee brother years ago at football training, and Diamond has been waiting all this time to get him. He heard the man was back in the area, and he broke in and beat him to a pulp with two hammers, then tied him up in his car and sprayed petrol round and set it going, and then he waited around with a tape recorder and taped him screaming and begging to be shot, so he could play it back to his wee brother. That's what I heard, anyway.'

'Sounds like the very man we need. Get him stirred up. Jack, away down and tell him I said he's a traitor and a yellow chicken for going solo.'

'No fucking way. If you seen some of the stuff he done.'

'He won't say nothing to you. He knows how I operate. A boy like that just needs a wee nudge. Get his engine lit. He'll be up, I guarantee.'

'You better be fucking right.'

'I am always fucking right. And here, see if he'll bring thon tape.'

33

Diamond McDaid could still see the face of the Brit who'd held a gun to his da's head. The things he made him say. Laughing with the rest of the soldiers.

He was only twelve at the time. His father wouldn't look him in the eye for a week after. Next time he did, he beat the tar out of him. He was never the same. Some wee cog knocked out of joint.

Diamond hadn't had a day of his life since that he wasn't burning with rage for that. Not at his da. At the soldier.

It was why he joined the Ra. The only reason.

He'd have loved an all-out war. That's what he wanted most of all. He watched the old films, the Roman ones, the cowboy ones, the World War Two ones. He had all the videos. John Wayne. Charlton Heston. Stallone. Chuck Norris. He went to see *Braveheart*, again and again. He thought about running at the English with spears and swords. Hacking at their heads. Getting his blade in the guts of a man who'd come out to meet you, fair and square, watching his eyes as he died in front of you, the black leaking down inside his eyes, knowing you'd killed him, him knowing you'd killed him, you'd pull him close in and whisper in his ear exactly why you'd killed him, he would die knowing that. Nobody else would hear, but just the fact of you doing that made the world a harder place, a nastier place, a crueller place. The poison leaked out. That was all he wanted. That was what made him get out of bed in the morning. Make the Brits suffer what he had suffered.

Most of all he'd have loved to take on the higher-ups. He imagined them all, London and Dublin both, out in the field, and him chasing them. He'd slice them and they wouldn't forget it. See if there was red blood or pish-water in their veins.

A sword. Up at Stormont where they were having the talks. Aye, that was it. Straight into the middle of them with a fucking samurai sword. He slowed it right down, took his time. Frame by frame, like a Bruce Lee video. Running at the first one, swish, swish, open his chest, open his neck. Pishing blood. Push him out of the way. He wouldn't be doing any more talking. The next one ran at him, and chop down, hard, just to one side of the head. Halfway through his shoulder. Took a good tug to get the sword out. They were all fumbling and stumbling and trying to call for the peelers. Meanwhile he was slashing and cutting. Opening up faces, opening up guts. Blood blood blood blood. So much fucking blood. Gallons of the stuff. Like the gunge tank on Noel Edmonds. Sploshing over everybody and everything. Pouring out all over him. Wearing it like a second skin. He felt like it was washing him clean. English blood leaking into Irish soil. That made him happy. Fuck yes.

But he'd go at the Dublin ones too. Damn sure. They were nearly worse. Selling out their own people for a pat on the head from the Queen. One of them ran at him, a big fat slabber. He swooshed low with the sword, cut the legs out from under him. Chop. Took the head off the next one, a narrow wee ferrety-looking boy. Bosh. Got another in the face with the butt, and then cut him longways near in half as he went down, from his nuts to his neck. Stopping to make a smart remark after every one, like James Bond. He hasn't a leg to stand on. Put this on your chopping list. He's not half the man he used to be. All that.

He imagined a load of Brits training in England, somewhere they weren't guarded. He was in the woods nearby. No, up on a hill, watching them. He'd got a fucking great spear. He flung it from ages away. Watched it swooshing. They all saw it before it landed. Lifted up their big round shields. But it went straight through. Right into his chest and out the back, pinned the bastard to the ground. Then he had to raise up his own shield and let them have a go at him. The spear hit bang in the middle, ripped right through, but he turned his body round and it only scratched him.

Then they ran at each other with swords. Sharp as a razor, flinging it about like a hurley stick. If you didn't go all out, you were done for. The winner was the one who wasn't afraid of dying. Simple as that. And that was him.

Those must have been the fucking days. May the best man win. And he would win, every time. Because his cause was right. He knew it. And they knew it too.

He didn't need asked twice. He was in.

34

Dog hated being wounded. All the sitting around. Fuck all to do. He always ended up thinking. And he really hated thinking.

There was one particular incident always went round and round Dog's head, was it the right thing to do. And the trouble was, that started him thinking was the whole thing the right thing to do. If all them ones on the TV that called men like him a thug and a heartless monster knew the half of what was in his head. Tore himself up some nights with guilt and worry.

It was right after his da died. He couldn't sit still in them days. Climbing the walls. Out and about. Looking for trouble. Itching for something.

One evening he saw a car he didn't know parked at the back of Dumbo's. A maroon Sierra, but there was something about it. Looked too new to be as old as it looked.

He dandered over, had a gander. Spotted the weld marks. Armour plating.

A plain-clothes cop would have more wit. Undercover Brit for sure.

He stepped into Dumbo's, ordered a pint. Nodded at a few old heads. Knew most of the young lads to see. A couple of tourists, poor fuckers. Talking too loud, laughing too hard.

And this one fella on a low stool at a wee round table in the back, reading his paper.

Dog watched him. The fella didn't turn a page. Kept his head down. He was listening. Army intelligence. Dog was sure of it.

Said nothing. Waited.

The fella kept glancing at the bog door. It was busy enough in there. A lot of coming and going. Maybe one of the young lads dealing a bit of speed or puff. Any other night Dog might have gone in and knocked heads. Not tonight.

It quietened down. The young lads were gathering themselves to head on. When the last one who'd gone in had come out, the fella he was watching got up and went in to the bog himself. He'd waited till it was clear. Dog waited too.

The fella came back. He was fiddling and footering with something in his pocket. A radio, or a mobile phone. Reporting back what he heard, or just saying he's all done. A pager, maybe, telling him to get back to base.

Right enough, the fella left the bar. Didn't finish his pint. Amateur, thought Dog. That's day one. Who doesn't finish their pint?

Dog waited a beat, one, two, three, then left after him.

The fella was in his car. Dog walked over, tapped the window.

Nothing.

Tapped again.

He could near hear the fella thinking. Down it came.

'Excuse me, I wonder could you offer me a lift down the road? I've had a few too many this evening and I better not drive. In case the army stop me. You know? The army.'

Nothing.

'I said, the army can be tricky fuckers when they want to be. You know?'

Nothing.

'It's not far, but I don't want to walk. The road's black, and the way some of them drive around here, I'd be a corpse by morning. Only if it's no bother to you, mind. I don't want to give a gentleman like yourself the slightest bit of bother.'

The fella shook his head, leaned over and opened the passenger door. Cautious, but friendly enough. In sat Dog. Off they driv.

'You're not from round here,' says Dog. The man mumbled and grunted a no.

'Is that an English accent?' says Dog. 'You've nothing to worry about. I have no beef with the English.'

'That's always nice to hear,' says the man. Pure Brit.

'So what has you in this part of the world?'

'I'm a tourist, I suppose you might say. Family history. I'm rather hoping to find a few graves.'

'Are youse English at that crack now?' says Dog. 'I thought it was only the Yanks fell for that lark.'

'I'm interested,' says the fella. 'It's something of a hobby of mine.'

'Well you've come to the right place,' says Dog. 'Graves is one thing we have plenty of.'

Nothing.

'No shortage of graves round here. That's one department where we allow no slacking.'

Nothing.

'Old graves and new graves, fancy graves and manky graves. Even a few unmarked graves, so they say. Oh, yes, graves is one thing that'll never go out of fashion in this here neck of the woods, I can guarantee you that. We do love digging ourselves a nice wee grave.'

Nothing.

'Just pull in here, would you,' says Dog. 'That'll do rightly.'

Stepped out, and then leant his head back in.

'I'll see you about.' The man nodded.

'I said, I'll see you about.'

Nodded again. Drove off, a wee bit too fast. Just a wee bit too fast.

In home, Dog sat in his kitchen. Had a think.

Family history. A cool customer. Could be true. Could be a lot of things.

He just wasn't sure enough for a bullet. No interest in killing an innocent man.

To tell you the truth, Dog hated killing. But he told himself that made him even more of a hero for doing it when it was needed. Pig was right, what he always said. There was no glory in doing what you love doing, even for a righteous cause. It's the ones who offer to do what they can't stand doing we should be grateful to. Men like himself. Amen to that.

Dog put it about to the dickers to keep an eye on the same car. And sure enough, word came back the following night that it'd been seen again, acting a wee bit suspicious. Idling outside certain pubs and shops. Driving the same circuit over and over. The very same fella at the wheel. He even stopped and looked at the odd grave. A nice touch. Maybe not such an amateur after all.

Dog tailed the car himself, next time he got the word. Just half an hour, keeping his distance, stopping and starting, having a yarn with a few heads he knew along the way.

Next day he heard. It'd been spotted driving out from the barracks, after dark.

He headed out for a drive that night, and saw it himself, up at the shops. Gave it a wee tail. He had a feeling. Just a funny wee notion tonight might be one of them nights.

He didn't try and keep his distance. Wanted the fella to feel a bit of heat.

Right enough, he started to put the foot down. Dog did the same. Make him nervous. Let him know we're on to him. Maybe force an error. At worst, get them worried, change their MO. Chuck out weeks and months of work. That thought made him smile.

The boy was rallying along now. Dog revved his own. A few tight corners coming up. Dog had raced along here a hundred times. He knew every bend, every pothole. Keep the pressure on. The fella floored it and disappeared. Dog hung back.

He had a feeling. Just a wee feeling.

Jackpot. Round the next corner, and the car was in the

ditch. Dog let out a wee yo-ho. His lucky night all right. The bastard had missed the sharp bend by the holy well, and he was halfway up the hedge. There'd be a chopper out to take him back in five minutes, Dog had to work fast. Stopped the car, and up out. A big moon, so they could see each other well enough.

The man was out of the car now too. Bruised up, nose bashed in, the trousers tore on him and skinned along one leg, but nothing too serious.

'Can I give you a hand there?'

'Ah, oh. Fuck.' He was trying to stand, but something was hurting him bad. 'Well, that's jolly decent of you. Fuck fuck fuck. I'll call someone. They'll be along in a moment. I don't want to hold you up.'

'There's nothing I'd rather do,' says Dog. 'Nowhere I'd rather be.'

'Really, it's best you leave me be. I need to call someone.'

'I'd say you do. The thing is, but, I had your number the first time I seen you. That night you gave me a wee lift. I'm sure you knew who I was, and I had a damn good idea who you were too. Hard luck, old bean.'

The fella changed his tone. Hard as nails all of a sudden.

'Listen, Campbell. There'll be serious shit if you mess around with me.'

'You took the words right out of my mouth,' says Dog. He popped the boot. 'In.'

And the tune changed again. What little colour was in the boy's cheeks had gone out of there.

'Christ. No no no. Not this. Not now. Please.'

'I won't tell you again.'

'No no no. Listen. Listen. How much? Do you understand me? How much? My family is rich, I guarantee you. Whatever you want.'

'Save it,' says Dog. 'In, this second, or I'll do you right here on the spot.'

Dog driv him up to Granny Duff's place. Deaf as a post, so a handy wee standby.

Backed the car up to the doors of the old van. Opened them up. Opened the boot.

Your man was weeping like a woman.

'Away to fuck out of that and in the back of the van. Call yourself a soldier.'

Dog hopped in too, shut the doors over. The wee light on. He could hear the fella breathing like a bull. Calm now. Calmer, anyway. But still snivelling.

'Fuck sake. Here's a tissue. Clean yourself up. Have a bit of self-respect.'

'Thank you, thanks. Sorry. Sorry.'

'What's that smell? Have you shat yourself?'

'I think I have. Adrenaline. I'm sorry.'

'Jesus Christ. I can pick 'em.'

But your man started babbling.

'Look here. I want no trouble. The thing is, I'm finished with the army, okay? I can't take it, and that's the truth. This sort of business. You bloody people. I've already resigned my commission. This was supposed to be my last tour. Do you understand? All I want is to go home, take over my father's business. He's bloody rich.' He let that sit for a minute. 'Do you understand me? I mean properly wealthy.'

'He'll have to be, to get you out of this one.'

And now he was all biz, hopping up and down.

'Yes! Yes he is! How much do you want? I'm serious! I'll arrange it right now. Right now. A cheque, made out to you, personally. No, that's bullshit. Sorry. Sorry. Listen. Okay. Let me think, just let me think for a second, okay? Okay?'

Dog let him think.

'Right. Listen. I can have cash here tomorrow. Just one signature, one phone call, and they'll transfer as much as you like. No one'll ever know. An offshore account set up in your name. I don't care what you do with it. I mean thousands. Tens of thousands. Name your price.'

'A hundred grand.'

'It's yours! It's yours! Take me tonight, no, wait, keep me here tonight, take me straight to the bank tomorrow, wear a suit, I'll explain you're a business partner, up to Belfast, Bangor, somewhere no one knows you. Or we can take the ferry to Scotland, and you leave me behind when we've finished. Anywhere. I'll have the money, in cash, in your hands by noon tomorrow. One hundred thousand pounds. That's a promise. You have my word. You have my solemn word. On my mother's grave. Bring a bloody big bag, that's all.'

'Are you for real?'

'It's only money. For Christ's sake. It's only money. This is my life we're talking about. This is my life. Take the lot. Take the lot. It's yours.'

He was tempted. Fuck it, why not? If the Brit really was on his way out, then he wasn't even a soldier any more, kind of. They were off-limits when they'd left the forces. We have to be better than them, he thought, or else what are we fighting for? He was no savage, he was a soldier too. He felt it deep. Not often he did, but he did tonight. The man was unarmed. It should be a fair fight.

He heard a car pull up. Then a wee rap at the van door. He knew the rhythm. Tap tap tap tap, ta-tap tap tap tap, tap tap, ta-tap tap tap. *Match of the Day*. His big brother, their way of knowing each other since they were boys. They'd whistle it, or hum it, or tap it like now, to let the other know it was him.

Dog opened the door a crack.

'Get in, quick.'

The door was pulled open wide. He could smell Pig before he saw him. The stench of sows off him. Smuggling. A border run. Switching tags.

'The fuck are you playing at, you prick? I've been looking you half the night.'

'This here Brit. Just sorting out a wee matter.'

Pig shut the door behind him nice and easy, took in the scene.

'Fuck me, you landed one. Fair play to you, boy.'

'Better than that. He's going to set us up, me and you. Rich da. We let him run on, and it's fifty grand. Two of us split it down the middle, say nothing to nobody.'

Dog glared at the Brit, dared him to squeak. The man was agog, but he kept schtum.

'Well, aren't we the lucky pair. And here, what happens the Brit?'

'Say we interrogated him and then he got away. What difference? Say any old shite. Say nothing at all, pretend it never happened. He's not armed, he's on his way home. He seen nothing. He knows who we are anyway, there's nothing new there. We're just having a yarn. He says any different, we can always sort him out again, sort his family out.'

'Listen, Dog. Listen here a minute. Did any of them ever let you run on?'

'But if he stumps up the cash. Fair's fair.'

'Fair? God give me strength. And I suppose they treated you fair when you were in Gough Barracks, did they? Stroked your head and gave you tea and buns? Or did they not beat the tar out of you with steel toecaps, and then piss in your face, and then throw a plastic bag full of the squaddie you'd booby-trapped into the cell with you for the night? Because that's what they fucking did with me.'

'Aye, I know, but the money.'

'Don't be a sap. What do you want with money? What are you short of? Have you debts I don't know about? But no matter if you do. You need money, then you make it or you take it, same as the rest of us.'

'Even so. It's not right to just empty him.'

'I tell you this. And listen to me now, so you learn something for once. If that there man was a woman, nine months pregnant with a wean that would grow up to be a soldier, I'd say the fucking same. A bullet in the belly would be good enough for her. Sit and wait for the ba to come out and then stave in the tiny wee skull with a half-brick, sooner than let another Brit grow up thinking it's his duty to come here and walk all over my country like he owns it. Any Irishman who'd do different has no fucking pride. And most of them do have no fucking pride, more shame to them. But not my own brother. Not my own wee brother. The only good Brit in this here county, while it's under the union jackboot, is a dead Brit. You know it and I know it. So let's make extra fucking sure this one is a good Brit.'

Dog pushed the man back and stepped away. No point arguing with Pig when he was in this kind of form. He gave the fella a wee shrug. Tried my best, but what can you do?

'If you're trying to scare me, it's fucking working,' says the man. 'Christ. Anything you want, both of you. Name your price.'

Pig stuck his short in the man's nose and banged off a round. Then another. Then another.

'I hate that smug superior sneering noise out of their fat English gobs.'

An awful mess. The whole front of his head was gone. Lumps of white jelly dropping out. Dog picked half a lip off his jumper. It was fucking disgusting. He hated this part.

Pig scraped red gunk out of the end of his barrel.

'Meat,' he says. 'We're all just meat. Do you ever think that?'

'Not really.'

'Naw, you never think nothing, do you? It's as well I'm here to do your thinking for you. Come on.'

'What do we do with the van?'

'Drive it down to the quarry and torch it.'

'With him in it?'

'The fuck do I care? Think for yourself for once in your life. Get rid of the forensics but make sure they know it was us. Or dump him at the cross-roads with a dummy device, so everybody has a good squizz before they can get mopping him up. Now come on and clean yourself before it's light. You look like a fucking knacker.'

35

One night the next week, when he was back on his feet, Dog told Diamond McDaid the story, up at the Ships. All except the fifty-grand part. He needed somebody to say it was the right thing to do, and Diamond was a safe bet. The cruellest cunt he knew.

Diamond gave a wee whistle after.

'It can be a hard call, right enough. I mind the like of that happened me one time.'

And Dog pulled in his chair. He needed a break from this shite going round his head all day. Rare enough too for Diamond to come out with a good yarn.

'This is years ago. I got called in to do a Brit they'd finished interrogating,' says Diamond. 'Just a squaddie, but still. The boy who was supposed to do it got lifted on his way up. Wait now till I tell you. And this is to go no further. I mean that.

'They left me alone with him. Said he hadn't run. Put up a decent fight. Told them nothing, even after a fucking good hiding. I was to finish him off.

'Boys, but he was in a bad way. Tied wrists and ankles. Half his teeth gone. I didn't look too close at his fingers, but I'd say he wouldn't be biting his nails any time soon.

A lot of fag burns. Keks down, and his ballbag swelled up to twice the size. Bad.

'But he was smiling. Some kiddo.

'How are you doing there, says I. Just to break the ice, you know. I've had worse Saturday nights, says he. And I had to laugh. Turns out he was Scotch. From Glasgow, he told me. A Rangers man. Better than that, he told me he had the top on under his uniform. Away or that, says I. But I had a look, and right enough, there it was. I wear it for luck, says he. I had to fucking laugh again. And he did this time and all.

'He was all right. Some of them are, if you get them on their own.

'I told him I was a Celtic man, and he says, no fucking shite. We had to laugh again. The bhoys and the huns, with our own wee derby. And looks like it's your day, he says. Hampden in the Sun all over again.

'I was made up. Couldn't stop grinning. Do you know what he meant? Not a Celtic fan? Call yourself Ra. Fuck sake. Seven Past Niven. Mean nothing? Well wait till you hear.

'This was donkey's ago. Fifty-seven or fifty-eight, I forget just now. The League Cup final. The Rangers were riding high in them days and the Celts couldn't get near them. We had good players, mind. A few great ones. Sean Fallon, from Sligo. Billy McPhail. Neilly Mochan, the Smiler. But the manager was no damn good. The board were picking the team, and chopping and changing every turn round, depending on who the chairman liked the look of.

'But that day. It was lovely weather, and everybody was in great form, my granda says. He was over working in Glasgow, and he was mad for the Hoops, like my da, like myself. He'd tell you great stories about them days. You'd nearly feel like you'd been there yourself. Up on the red tram, number nine, with the players riding alongside. You'd see them all coming out on the pitch then, and you'd tell each other who you'd seen doing what. You'd run through the other side too, which one was a pushover, which one you'd need to watch out for. You didn't want to miss a thing, for at home they'd want every detail told and told again. Valentine, the new lad for the Blues, nobody knew what to think about him.

'And the sun was out. October, but it was like a holiday. Something clicked that day. Two before half time, and five more after. A massacre. Seven to one. Sammy Wilson opened the account. A hat-trick for McPhail in the second half, all on the head. Valentine, the new lad, he had a bad day. Dick Beattie our goalie with his seven fingers in the air. A bit of a character.

'My granda said it was the happiest he'd ever been in his life. Just to knock the budgie off its perch. He was over with a crowd from Belfast working on the docks. He said it made him proud to be Irish that day.

'But listen till you hear, now. My granda said him and his mates near got a hiding from a crowd of young Blues, but a couple of old-timers chased them, and told the lads well done for the game, fair fucks to youse. And him and his mates ended up drinking that night with a whole bunch of Rangers fans, and they bought every pint, and said he was a sound lad. They swapped oul yarns about matches and derbys and who'd been at what game, and which players they fancied and which they couldn't wait to see the back of.

'And wait till you hear. The Brit, the Scotchie, he says then that his granda was at that game and all. Would you believe that? What are the chances? And the Celts deserved every goal and more besides, his granda said. A die-hard Rangers man, but any time he talked about that day, he said he had to hand it to the Celts, that was one of the best ninety minutes of football he'd ever seen in his life. Any time any of his mates laid in too hard with the banter, he'd speak up for the Hoops in that cup final. Do you ever hear the like? A die-hard Rangers man. Even the penalty right in the dying moments. Something to see. He said his granda couldn't help smiling at work the next week, seeing Catholic mates of his so happy, at this wee uplift give to half the town when things were tough. He knew the Rangers weren't beat, they'd come back up again, so we could spare the one win, he said. But what a win. Seven to one. Straight up.

'And wait till you hear. The Brit told me his granda went drinking with a wee gang of Celtic fans that night. Maybe it was my granda and his granda having a pint, what do you think about that? And when the old timers chased the young bucks and took him drinking with a crowd of huns and bought him pints all night, maybe that was his granda among them. Imagine that.

'And now here was the two of us.

'Listen to me, says I. Am I fuck plugging you. You have your colours on, and I might as well tell you, I have mine on and all. Look there. And I showed him my top, under my jumper. I never go out on a job without it. I swear there was a fucking tear in my eye, and that hadn't happened this years. For anything.

'Give me that shield off your shirt, says I, and I'll give you mine here. I'll pin on your Rangers crest next time I'm out and you wear the Celtic one under your kit and we'll see which brings who good luck. If your granda might have saved my granda from getting a hiding, and bought him pints after losing a derby, then you're a sound man as far as I'm concerned. Get away to fuck out of this and we'll say no more about it.

'And wait till you hear what he said. Wait till you fucking hear.

'Will you not get in trouble?

'Some kiddo. I tell you what.

'Don't you worry your wee head about that, says I. Just count your blessings it fell out the way it did. Away on now before I change my mind.

'So there you are. That's what happened me. Some fucking crack, eh? Just goes to show, you never do know. Best not to think too hard about it.

'I've to head on here, but I'll say this before I go. Thinking gets you nowhere in this game. That's my opinion, anyway. Crack on with the job, and leave the brain-work to the higher-ups. Good luck, now. Keep her country.'

Henry

36

When you hear some of the stories, you can see plain that the old times were not a bit different than today. This here was always a handy spot to billet an army. First was the old plantation castle, near four hundred year old, but only the bare stony walls of that were left. Around the back of there had been the RIC station a hundred years ago, and then they put up a whole tin city for Yanks waiting to take on the Nazis. Because of this land at the rear, and because it was so close to the border, they took the place up when the whole thing kicked off as one of the big bases, and built it up over the twenty-odd years.

The ruin itself was Castle William, and the base often got called the same. If you didn't know it already, big letters bolted to the front of the old castle told you, for there was a sort of a tourist trail took you past this way, though few enough ever came. Some said the name was because King Billy stayed there around the time of the Battle of the Boyne, or it was named in his honour when he became the King of England. Others said it was because a man called Fitzwilliam had it built, but the Fitz had been dropped over time. You could take all these yarns with a pinch of salt, but at the same time, nobody would dispute that every

Michael Hughes

story had some wee bit of truth at the back of it. Take your pick, or come up with your own.

A few years back some lads coming home from the Glenallen tried to wreck the sign, feeling affronted I suppose that the place was known only as a British garrison, as if that was a great thing, but they got no further than pulling down the W before they got fed up or somebody chased them. From that day on the sign said Castle Illiam, and the young fellas around the town had started calling the base itself Illiam, just for the crack, and to wind up the peelers and the soldiers. It kind of caught on for a while there.

Not a one of the locals had ever been inside. It was the biggest building anywhere near, you couldn't miss it, it hung over the whole country around, but the inside of it was a big black nothing to them. They didn't know the name of a single one of the men who lived there.

37

Now we're getting to it. Wait till you hear. This one individual in particular. The only man the squad were afeard of, though they never knew his name till after. Only what he'd done. Henry Morrow. A captain in the SAS. An exceptional individual, everybody said so. One of a kind. They were lucky to have him, down here in the back of beyond.

He'd had his first taste of action in the Falklands, when he was fresh into 2 Para, straight out of training. Savage bastards they were, raring to fight, gumming to kill. And kill they did. Young Henry was up there with the worst of them. Five Argentines himself at Goose Green. No mercy. He was full of the fight, champing at the bit. He was a machine. He was fearless. The best of the best. He'd found his people.

He was well decorated, and the brass took note. Nudged him towards Special Forces, along with a fair number of his comrades. The SAS was bulging with Paras in them days, with their old NCOs training them up in Hereford, for there were few enough about who had experience of that kind of action. And you never knew where it would blow up next.

Except you did. Northern Ireland was a guaranteed stop, and Henry had been over and back a few times now, doing full-year tours round the border. The SAS was a different kettle of fish. They could be savage, for sure, but they weren't mad for it, like the Paras. They were all about stealth, and cunning. Finding the smart way to do what you needed to do, and do it quietly. Invisible. Tough, yes, none tougher. But clever with it. He'd spent endless hours waiting in close observation for Ra men who never showed up, eating dry rations, shitting in bags, and it taught him the value of patience. He learned there was more than one way to skin a cat. There was so much to learn.

And plenty to forget. There were things he'd seen and heard he would never tell another living soul. Stuff he wouldn't know how to start to describe. Things he'd done himself, that made his stomach cramp and his head spin when he thought about them. So he didn't think about them.

But like any man who got to be the best at what he did, they promoted him off that job, and sat him in a wee office directing others who weren't half as good. He was a captain now, and captains hardly ever went in the field these days. They couldn't afford to lose one. That kind of experience didn't come cheap.

And his men loved him. Do anything for him. Straight, and fair, and he'd back them to the hilt. Six foot three, a big shock of red hair, a wee splash of freckles on each cheek. When he'd go in undercover, the men used to joke that he was so convincing as Irish, that maybe he was really one of the bad guys, undercover in the SAS.

He didn't hate the locals, but. He didn't hate the Irish

at all, not even the IRA. He understood. He was an educated man. He'd read his history. And he wanted to be a small part of that history himself. The stuff he'd always loved was the battles, the bloodier the better. His bedroom used to be strewn with wee soldiers and horses and castles. That was where history was made. Standing up to fight for your country. It was all he'd ever wanted to do.

Now he'd married, and had a child of his own, he saw things a wee bit different. Looking at anybody now, he couldn't help seeing the baby they used to be. That helped, and it didn't. But there you are. He was still learning.

When it came down to it, he didn't agree with being in Northern Ireland. In the officers' mess, he'd argue the bit out, until the brass told him to wise up, for fear of damaging morale. He got the message.

But he loved being in the thick of it. He never got tired of that. A pig in shite. He was a knight. He was a redcoat. He was up flying a Spitfire. Doing the very same job, as the times demanded. He was the line of civilisation, standing at the edge of what Britain was supposed to be about, holding back the chaos, taking on the enemy. He was old-fashioned, he knew, but he prided himself on that.

And if the promotion didn't suit him, then neither did the ceasefire. He was climbing the walls at Bessbrook Mill, itching for action. The old cogs getting rusty. He had no doubt there were evil bastards among the Provos, and all he wanted was a chance to take them out.

In particular, the famous Border Sniper. That was the scalp he craved above all. It drove him mad that one man could so frighten the brass that they'd changed their whole MO in the area. It should be the other way round. He wanted a chance to prove the point. Some bastards weren't worth arresting. There was only one language they understood.

He heard Bernard King was over now, a Para colonel he'd served under, newly in charge down round the border, and he put out feelers to see if he could get his hands dirty again. Bernard was only too happy to oblige.

There was something brewing in the area. Special Branch and the army had been running the wife of a local player as an agent, Bernard told him. In the months running up to the ceasefire, they'd thwarted just about every operation the local ASU had set up. But the husband had started to get suspicious, so they'd pulled her out. It had all been rather messy. Apparently she'd got a bit too friendly with her handler. And the handler himself had got cold feet, for fear she was working both sides and the player might be on to him now, so he'd put in for a transfer, fled away off to some cushy number in Germany. Out the same day on a Chinook, straight up in the air and then dropped down in a nice comfy bed. He had connections, so they said. The higher-ups wanted him out of harm's way. The woman wanted nothing more to do with him, once she got wind he was running scared. She was long gone, set up with a new life on the mainland, but they were still trying to untangle the legal issues. The whole thing was a shambles.

But she'd given some spot-on intel on the local players, and Bernard wanted Henry out and about, keeping an eye.

Henry jumped at it. But Bernard had a warning for him. 'The last chap we had watching this lot came a cropper. It was hushed up, wheels within wheels, but you have to be aware, we're dealing with savages.

'And the clock's ticking. We think the local ASU here is planning to break the ceasefire, and the Army Council are leaning their way. Sinn Fein are very torn about it. On the one hand, if they come down heavily they risk splitting the movement, and avoiding that is their absolute top priority. Ahead of peace, probably ahead of a united Ireland, if you ask me. But on the other hand, if they let it go ahead, it looks like they've been dicking us around.'

'I thought Sinn Fein pulled the strings.'

'When the wind is southerly. This place is a bloody cat's cradle, don't you think? Everyone's got a string and everyone's pulling it like crazy, just to see what's on the end.'

'Dare I ask who's pulling our string?'

'Well, quite. So here it is. After that unfortunate incident a few weeks ago, the Barry Ross business, we still hoped things could hold, and they have. Loose cannons on both sides, excusable given the circumstances. Under the carpet. Needless to say there's been a lot of back-channel activity, and both sides say they're desperate for the thing to work. I believe the local unionist chap has been talking directly with Sinn Fein, very hush-hush, trying to find a way through. But the NIO are worried about what PIRA might be up to, and they're fed up with guesswork from us. Local knowledge is key. Man to man. Do you see what I'm getting at?'

'I'm afraid I don't, quite.'

'Well, look. Right now, our greatest frustration is that we don't have a direct link here on the ground. The usual chap they were willing to deal with as and when has retired, and the MOD are dragging their heels on a replacement. But the NIO wants to start that up again pronto, so we need a volunteer to make initial contact, suss out someone in the area willing to engage. Not to negotiate, I want to emphasise that. Just to hear what they say they want, and make a few educated guesses as to their thinking. We know they don't trust the civil servants. They don't trust the new London people. We think they'll respond best to green army, someone who talks their language.'

'When?'

'Today. Right now. Before the wind changes. You know what the weather's like in this bloody place. For all I know it might already be too late, but we have to try. The fact is, we have to take this ASU out of the picture, one way or another. It's a genuine obstacle to peace, both sides know it.

'Look, it might come to nothing. It might be one meeting. But their usual trigger man, a cold bastard, is off the scene, so I've been told. Some kind of internal squabble. Yes, the mythical sniper is real, apparently. Which gives us an opening.

'Worst-case scenario, it goes nowhere, and we're back to bang-bang. Plan B is to catch them in the act, and take them out. We have enough decent intel to make that a goer. But in the meantime, it might be that little bit harder next time for one of them to slot one of us, if he's spent an hour talking man to man.'

'Aren't you concerned the same thing might apply to me?'

Was that the tiniest of smiles?

'No, Henry, I'm not. Should I be?'

38

He got himself up in green-army gear. Thick streaks of camo cream on his face, green and brown and black. Kevlar helmet with the visor down. Scrim scarf tight around his gob. His own ma wouldn't know it was him.

Waited in the back of the Land Rover, while the boys set up the VCP. Pelting with rain. It sounded like a riot.

Right now, he was aching for a proper riot. Lead a snatch squad into the thick of it, pick up a couple of the players, give them a good going over in the back of a Saracen. That was the way it used to be done, and it bloody well kept them in order. Everybody was walking on eggshells these days. Waste of time.

His radio crackled. 'He's here, sir.'

Henry watched out of the hinged flap. Shane Campbell was always very civil to the soldiers, much more so than to his own side. More to lose. And always clean as a whistle.

He could see the squaddie leaning in. Would you mind stepping this way, sir. One of the officers just wants to have a word. No sign of movement. He sensed a bit of tension. Not today, thank you.

Down to the car himself. Sent the squaddie off out of earshot. 'Mr Campbell. I know you're a busy man, so I'll get straight to the point. There's a lot of interest on our side in the noises coming from your side. Mixed messages, to say the least. The suggestion has come up that a couple of us get together, to explore if there's anything worth exploring, to try to keep things on an even keel. Is there someone who'd be willing to come in? It might go nowhere, but it's better than taking pot-shots, don't you agree? All above board. We make it look like an arrest, just giving you low-level hassle, the usual thing. Once he's in, whoever it is, he just talks. We listen. We'll be here again tomorrow evening, same time, and if we see a familiar face, we'll proceed from there. I'll leave it with you.'

Campbell didn't move, didn't even acknowledge him. Henry didn't wait for an answer, just slapped the bonnet smartly, twice. The squaddie on the road stepped back, and the car drove on.

39

Back at the base, Henry got pulled aside when he stepped out of his vehicle.

'Phone for you. Compassionate. Urgent, she says.' He went to receive it.

'Hello, my precious. It's your mother here. We're all concerned about Anna. She isn't at all well. We think you ought to take a little time. You can ask for compassionate.'

'Actually, Mother, I can't. Things are at a crucial stage.'

'Things are always at a crucial stage. You sound just like your father, you know. You men take yourselves far too seriously. Have a drink, for God's sake. Learn to relax once in a while.'

'I'm on ops, Mother. I haven't washed or changed in days. I'll take time off when I have time off. I can't just have a nice sit-down when I feel the urge.'

'Goodness. Don't blame me, Henry. What can I do?'

'If your peace movement has any connections with Sinn Fein, you could ask them to keep their rogue elements in check. How about that? That might help.'

'You know what's best, I'm sure. My son is a fine man. But think of your own son. His mother is in a pretty bad way.'

'Where is she?'

'That's just it. She took a plane to Belfast this morning,

with the boy. The nanny point-blank refused to come, so she's on her own with him.'

'Christ. What's she playing at?'

'Don't ask me. She said it was very urgent, and she had to tell you in person.'

'Stupid cow.'

'Just see her, Henry. Please.'

He checked the roster. He was already listed as on emergency leave. They didn't muck about. While he had the chance, he ought to go.

There was a transport heading up that way. He tagged along, still in green-army gear. Another kind of blending in. And he liked it. He felt like a soldier again.

At the married quarters, he waved his pass, checked where they'd put her.

He saw the whole place through her eyes, for once. The dull, depressing little flats. No wonder she'd stayed in Holland Park.

'Hello?'

Nothing. No, hang on. Was that a telly?

There she was, in the living room. Flicking between the channels. Those dreadful Sky people, the new World Service channel, and American cable news.

He sat beside, waited for her to speak. She didn't.

He said nothing. He knew the conversation would have a tripwire in it somewhere, and he was damned if he was going to pull it.

'Darling, is everything all right? I had a call from my mother.'

'Please. I'm watching this.'

He waited. She watched. He did too, for as long as he could stand it.

'She said you wanted to speak to me urgently. You could have phoned, you know.'

Nothing.

'Can't you leave the bloody news alone for five minutes?'

'Certainly not. I'm waiting to hear that they've killed you.'

Sod the kid gloves. He hadn't time for this.

'Oh, for Christ's sake, Anna. That's not very likely when I'm sat here, is it?'

He saw her lip wobble, but she caught it in time. Tossed her head, like she was shaking off a fly.

'You'll tell me I'm a fool, of course. That's your answer to everything. But I know, you see. I know you're going to die. There, I've said it.'

She'd tried this one before. Deep breath. Gently does it.

'We're all going to die, darling.'

She squeezed her eyes shut. Not the thing to say, clearly.

'Here. In this awful place.'

'I've seen worse.'

She almost smiled. That's the girl. Back on track.

'Quite. Just look at the world, Henry. There's so much death. So much killing.'

He looked. Inane trash. Cartoons for grown-ups.

'So much television, that's all there is. Cameras poking their noses in where they've no business. Seeing things we never have before, but it's a fraction of what's gone on in the past, believe me. Ignorance really is bliss sometimes.'

'You have a clever answer for everything.'

'Darling, listen to me. The Cold War is over. The Middle East is relatively stable. Yugoslavia looks like it's settling down, at last. And a ceasefire is coming here, mark my words. A permanent one. There really is no earthly reason to upset yourself. It's the safest time to be a British soldier for half a century.'

'You've always been the golden boy, haven't you? But what if no one's told the terrorists? You really think you're immune from those brutes, don't you? Sometimes I almost want it to happen, just to teach you a lesson.'

'What lesson? What are you talking about?'

'One day it'll be your name on that screen. Your beautiful face, smashed into pulp. I know it will, as surely as if it had already happened. I'm just waiting for the day. And when you die, why should I go on living?'

'Don't talk rot.'

'The IRA wants to kill you. That is their sole purpose, every single day. They've had plenty of practice, and they're very good at it. That's not rot, it's the truth.'

'Darling, they're on ceasefire. Their top people want peace now, just as much as we do. Probably even more. They're not brutes, and they're not idiots either. The main players are usually very serious, thoughtful individuals, believe it or not. They may use idiots and brutes to do their dirty work, but those idiots can't get anything done on their own. Just like in the army.'

'Well, be that as it may. I refuse to be party to it any longer. You must choose.'

'I'm sorry, now you really have lost me. What must I choose?'

'The army, or this family. Resign your commission after this tour.'

'Oh, don't be ridiculous.'

And that did it. Her voice rose in a wail, like a siren.

'It's driving me mad, Henry! It's very close to actually driving me mad!'

Fire with fire. The only way he knew.

Up on his feet, raise the volume.

'For Christ's sake, Anna! Don't you think I know all this? Don't you think it haunts me every night, lying awake fretting about you? Which I could do without, frankly. I have a duty, you know. These men have wives and children too. How could I face any of them if I wasn't prepared to take the same risks they take, every single day?'

'Henry, it's pointless. It's utterly futile. All those deaths were in vain. We have no right to be here.'

He sat. Took her quivering hands. Firm now. Look her in the eyes.

'That's just it, darling. That's what I'm trying to tell you, if you'll just give me the chance. Our boys are coming home from Ulster, perhaps very soon indeed. I'm certain of it. From a strategic point of view, you're quite right, all this was in vain. Of course it was. How could we possibly win? This is not our country, and it has the right to its own problems, and its own destiny. The sooner we can get out, the better.

'But you're not a child, and I won't treat you like one. Because you're right, you know. It might happen, darling.

The ceasefire might break down any day, we both know that. And it could all start again. And yes, it could be my face splashed on the news. Of course it could. That's the army. That's the SAS. I've never denied it.

'But hard as this will be to hear, I can live with that outcome. Do you hear me? I can cope with the thought of you living as a soldier's widow. What I can't accept is you living as a coward's wife. You think you'd prefer to have me home, but believe me, you don't want the person I would be if I took that course. And it would eat away at you too, that I shirked my duty. I know that perfectly well. It would eat away at Max, when he was old enough to understand. It would be known. I can't deny the man I am, for the sake of some silly anxiety of yours that I'm somehow doomed. None of us is doomed, darling. We make our own fate.

'But we can't just surrender. Do you realise what that would mean? Everything this country has built up over a thousand years, down in flames. Respect for democracy, the rule of law, facing down those who threaten those values. That's what it means to be British. If we surrender our principles, then they really have won. Well, I won't have it. I won't have my family held hostage to their twisted values at the point of a gun. I won't have you bring up our son in that world.'

'You said yourself we're going to pull out.'

'At the right time. That's up to the politicians. But no one will say I gave up the fight before we brought the bastards to heel. I serve my country, and I tell you I won't shirk my duty.'

'Sometimes we have conflicting duties.'

'That's perfectly true. I may not always get it right, but I do my best.'

'Is this your best?'

Up on his feet again. Christ, she was giving him the runaround today.

'Isn't it? Then tell me what I can give you, to make you happy!'

'A divorce, Henry.'

He laughed.

She didn't.

Nothing else to go on. Just the words.

He really didn't have the fucking time for this. Not today.

'This is the man you married, Anna. I haven't changed.'

'I see that now. I don't blame you, Henry. I made a mistake, that's all. It happens.'

'Christ. You're serious, aren't you?'

'You might inflict it on me, but you won't inflict it on our child. Not any more. The choice is entirely yours.'

He'd had enough. Time to call her bluff.

'I'm not making any choice, darling. You are. If that's what you have to do, I can respect your decision. But it is your decision, not mine. Don't you dare blame this on me.'

'Why are you always so defensive with me? I'm not your fucking mother!'

'No, but you're turning into yours! I don't want a row, you'll wake the baby.'

'He's not a baby any more. Unlike his father.'

'I can't do this now. Bad timing. I'm needed.'

'You're needed here.'

'Please, darling. I don't want to go like this.'

'We don't always get what we want, do we?'

He really had had enough now. Let her cool off. He couldn't have this nonsense fogging up his head. Not today.

'You need to buck up, for your own sake. People talk.'

He turned to the door, but she stood and gripped his arm.

'Henry! Don't you even want to see him?'

He didn't, but he couldn't begin to explain why. Not to her. He could taste the tang of the field. He was already crossing back.

'Quickly, then.'

She led him into the bedroom.

His little son there, asleep. The same freckles, the same thick red thatch.

Henry bent down.

'Max. Daddy's here.'

'Please don't wake him. He's been having night terrors.'

But the boy had woken. Startled eyes, rubbing away the sleep.

He saw the little lad see him. Piecing it together.

Henry lifted him. Face to face. And the boy opened his mouth, and screamed.

Screamed.

Screams to wake the dead.

Henry stroked his cheek, but the boy recoiled. The moment his hand connected, the shrieks redoubled. The purest terror.

'Shush! Please, Maxie, it's okay, it's Daddy! I came to see you.'

Fists and feet battered Henry. He took one full in the eye. The child was hysterical. He'd heard nothing like it outside the field.

'Christ. What's wrong with him?'

She touched his shoulder.

'It's your face, Henry. He doesn't know who you are.'

She was laughing now. A bloody good sign. He did too. He'd forgotten he was wearing the damn stuff, but he knew better than to say so. It might have been taken as meaning something.

He handed her the boy and pulled out his wipes, cleaned off the green and brown and black.

The boy saw Daddy's face, and the scream just stopped. Like a switch was flicked. In its place, the broadest gummy smile.

'Daddy. Daddy.'

He lifted the boy back from her. Held him high. She needed a display of affection. He gritted his teeth behind his own smile. Couldn't risk cracking the shell. Not today. Keep all that out.

'That's right. Good man. Up, up, up, see if you can touch the stars. Nearly. Nearly. Good effort. Soon you will. When you're big, like me.

'Now, listen. I want to say something. Look at me, Max. Are you listening? Good man. When you are big, like me, I want you to promise me something. Promise you won't stop there. I want you to outgrow me. Are you listening? Be a better man than I can manage to be. Be a better husband, and a better father, if you get the chance. Make your mother proud of you, as she can't always be proud of me. Do we have a deal?'

'Deal. Daddy deal.'

'That's the best I can offer you right now. One day I'll explain. One day, perhaps you'll find out for yourself.'

'Come home, Henry.'

'When the job is done.'

'One more chance. The last one.'

'That's the spirit.'

'I mean it this time. Oh, what's the use. I was an idiot to marry you.'

'That's hardly classified. I told you so at the time. Thank Christ you ignored me.'

He held her close. Both of them. Made himself, for her. Told himself he couldn't resist. Let himself feel it, just for a moment. Then wished he hadn't. Knew it was poison to the man he needed to be. Hoped she was happy now. Someone ought to be.

'It'll be over soon. Every war ends, and this is no exception.'

'Keep yourself away from trouble. Do your duty, but no more. Promise me that.'

'I promise you that. Now please, go home and wait. I'm coming back.'

'I won't wait for ever.'

'You won't have to. It's almost over.'

And then he closed that door. Turned away, looked away. Walked away.

Back to the war.

40

Pig presented it to the men.

Dog stepped up.

'Fuck it, I'll go. No bother. Let me get a look at the whites of their eyes. See how he justifies shooting down unarmed men going about their business. Arrogant pricks.'

'No,' says Pig. 'Not till you're a hundred per cent. We need a volunteer.'

They all looked at their hands. Scared it was a trap, or scared of looking like they were giving ground. Scared, anyhow.

Ned shook his old head, rattled out a cough.

'Youse should be ashamed of yourselves. Let me tell you a story here. In the Border Campaign, near forty years ago, we were asked to approach a notorious B-Special who had beat a wee woman round the head, and she was never the same after. Headaches, and then she died six months later, on a Christmas Eve. As good as murder. We all knew it was him, but the man was feared, and the peelers didn't want to know unless there was an official complaint. Well I stepped up. Not a one of them would step up, hard men all, but I did. I sat near an hour with that man, my sworn enemy, and tried to convince him to do the right thing. Turn himself in, and then there'd be no reprisals. Well, he wouldn't fucking listen, and he got what was coming to him soon enough. But if I was that age now, I'd be out the door ahead of any of you. And I will again, if none of youse have the guts.'

Straight off, five hands went up.

'That's liker it,' says Pig. 'Names-in-the-hat time. Any of you would be suitable.'

They all put their names on a fag paper, scrunched it up and dropped it in a bowl. Sid jiggled it about and then pulled one out.

He squinted at it.

'I can make nothing of that. Whose is it?'

He passed it round. Every man shook his head, until he got to Budd.

'That there's mine, so it is.'

'How does that say Jack?'

'It's a wee mark I use. My writing's not the best.'

Pig slapped him on the back.

'Good man yourself, Budd. You're the best of us, there's no doubt of that. No smart talk, no double-dealing, just head down and get on with the job, every time. You'll show them the true republican spirit. Don't take any shite.'

41

It happened just the way Henry said. Budd driv up to the checkpoint at the same time the next night, gave his name, and he got took up to the station. A peeler showed him into one of the interview rooms. The man wouldn't look him in the eye the whole time. Budd didn't mind. He understood well.

In the room, he waited. Happy enough. He could wait all night.

The Brit came in, dressed for patrol, except for the helmet. Snobby as fuck, Budd thought. But a fine-looking man apart from that. Big, broad, good head of red hair. He could pass for Irish. Probably he did, half the time.

'Thank you for giving up your time, Mr Hughes, and I'm sorry to have kept you waiting. I won't detain you any longer than is absolutely necessary.'

Henry felt his heart thump faster than it had any reason to. Perhaps this was lunacy, to try to engage with them. To let them get a good look at him. He hadn't expected Hughes. Why on earth had they sent him? He was a skilled operator, but not the brains of the bunch.

'We're aware that something is in the air locally. I'm here to ask you to please consider the implications of this very carefully. For yourselves, and for this country. There's a real opportunity at the moment, to engage with the political process and advance your cause that way. And I think you have every reason to hope that if you can make the argument, you will have your united Ireland in good time. But the people here don't want violence. They don't want you, frankly. You must know that. They want peace, and stability, and prosperity. And we would prefer to let you go about your business unmolested, your families and your associates. But that's not possible as things stand. To be plain, there's every possibility that an attempt to attack the military presence in the area will lead to a violent confrontation, and I'm afraid you're almost bound to come off worst.'

'I wouldn't say so.'

'I'm sorry?'

'I wouldn't be so sure we'd come off worst. Youse are so smug sitting in here. You might just get your comeuppance some day.'

'So there is something in the air?'

'There's nothing in the air but the smell of shite out of your mouth.'

'I won't say what we know, and I certainly won't say how we know it, but in this case I'm confident that our information is sound.'

'Is it Dog's woman?'

'Sorry?'

'Brian Campbell. Is it his wee wife Nellie that's been filling you in?'

'I'm afraid I don't know what you mean.'

'You soon will. That's all I'm saying.'

Henry felt tired. He wasn't cut out for this. Maybe Anna was right. Christ.

'Mr Hughes, let me ask you, man to man. We're sitting here, having a perfectly civil conversation. I mean, isn't this the better way? Taking us on is going nowhere. It's a bloody stalemate, a fool can see. Did you ever honestly think you'd be able to defeat us?'

The man shifted in his chair, looked him in the eye. He seemed to like what he saw.

'That's a straight question, and I'll give you a straight answer. We thought we could get you out, aye. We still do. Hit you hard enough, often enough, that you'll get your fill. For out you will get, sooner or later. That I do know.'

'I'm sure you're quite right. Declare a permanent ceasefire, engage with the political process, and we'll be out within weeks. But not before. That's our position. And let me add this. The IRA will lay down its weapons, sooner or later. And they will do it while Northern Ireland still exists. That I do know.'

'You might be right about that as well. But on our terms. We'd want a timetable for military withdrawal, within the lifetime of the parliament. An amnesty for prisoners and on-the-runs. The promise of reunification within a generation, and no unionist veto. A few other bits and pieces, but that'd do rightly.'

'We can't decide the outcome of negotiations in advance.'

'Certainly you can. You do it all the time. I watch the news.'

'We can't have your people as part of the talks until you declare a final ceasefire.'

'There's no way we pull the plug until we get a firm commitment to withdraw.'

'Well. Another stalemate. No shame in that. At least we're talking, eh?'

'Talk all you want. It gets us nowhere.'

'It stops us fighting.'

'Exactly. Gets us nowhere.'

The door opened, and a wee woman looked in. She nodded to Henry.

'Yes, Iris?'

She tapped at her wrist.

'Already?'

She gave a sharp nod, then left.

'I'm afraid it seems you're quite right, Mr Hughes. Other duties call.'

'You serious? We hardly got started.'

'Nonetheless. Shift-change here, and we have to call a halt. But, look. Man to man. I don't want this to be taken in the wrong spirit, but I'd like you to have this compass. No funny business, it's not bugged or anything, though I'm sure you'll have it checked out, and quite right too. Works perfectly well, I've used it myself in the field. A sort of souvenir of today, a token of our shared sense of direction for the future, something like that. So that in years to come, if perhaps your grandchildren ask you what the British Army were really like, this meeting might come to mind before some of your other encounters.'

'That's fair enough. I have nothing to give you, but. Unless, here. There you are. This is a Miraculous Medal. A true image of Our Lady of the Immaculate Conception. I don't know why I would want you to have good luck, but that's what it gives you. Just to show I have nothing against you personally, do you see. And so maybe indeed when your own children or your grandchildren ask you about the muck-savages there was in the Provos, you can say there was one man among them at least who had his mind on higher things.'

Pig

42

Pig was raging he didn't know. That was what hurt the most. Stabbed in the back. It was like they didn't trust him. Like everything he had done for his own side was turned to shite.

Canary Wharf, of all the targets to choose. Typical Belfast. Suits and ties attacking suits and ties. They knew nothing about how to fight. Driving out an occupying army.

Well he would show them. The gloves were off now.

But the needle was dug in his heart. Betrayed by the higher-ups. He was supposed to be the one to end the cessation, and they let that other crowd do it. Kept him in the dark. He felt like a total cunt in front of the squad. The whole townland.

The way the men looked at each other, and at him. He let on like he saw nothing. But he could hardly think straight, he was that worked up. One minute he felt like giving up, the next he wanted to take them on solo. The Brits and the Shinners both. All over the fucking place.

He called a squad meeting, up at the farm. The only way was to bull on regardless, with something, anything. Stay on the front foot.

But he was shit-scared too. He had an awful feeling his number was up. That they were coming for him. Fuck knows what they might have got out of young Nellie. She knew far too much. The whole thing was a massive balls-up.

It was time to call it. But he didn't know what. He wouldn't even know himself what he'd decided until he saw the rest of them sitting there, and opened his mouth to start talking.

43

What you need to understand is this. The Brits hadn't been out in numbers since Achill was on the job. They'd fly them in and fly them out, even to set up a checkpoint. On the roads was no-go completely. On foot, they'd only come out in multiples, eight or twelve at a time, and that was rare enough. The peelers wouldn't show their faces at all for weeks on end. The base had been Fort Apache for years.

Now they were out combing the place. Stopping every car. Redding through every farm. They saw their chance and they took it. No hiding place. They'd turn up every man hiding out, every bit of gear. They'd be recruiting touts left, right and centre. Everybody knew the score. If they got their teeth into this part of the country, there wasn't a hope.

But the truth was, if the half of the country knew what this squad were about, they'd be delighted to see them get lifted. People had got awful comfortable with the ceasefire. For the older ones, it was just back to normal. They'd never got used to the whole thing.

Even now, the whisper was about that it was coming back soon, and for good. People could smell it on the wind. Just imagine. No turning on the news in the morning half-braced for what you were going to hear. If it was a part-time member of the UDR you'd breathe a sigh of relief. Nothing serious. A terrible state of affairs, when you stop to think about it. Not the same checkpoints either. A wee taste of what it might be like, that was the idea. Most people liked it well. The tide was turning, is what it felt like. And it was a brave man who would set himself to turn it back the other way.

44

'There's going to be a statement from London.'

In the officers' mess, Henry and the usual few gathered around the TV. The others shrugged, a few didn't even look up from the pool table.

At the Ships, they switched off the TV, and turned on the radio. Nobody really thought about why they did that. Maybe they liked to see the looks on each other's faces as they listened. Take it in together.

In Holland Park, Anna had the radio on as she went over plans from the builders. It was time to start work on the old house. She'd give him something worth coming home to. The life they both deserved.

Up in Derry, a Sinn Feiner was meeting a man from MI5, just to exchange views. They both admitted they'd quite like to watch, to see what the other made of it.

Every one of them heard the measured voice, straining slightly, eager to please.

'We expect all sides to condemn this reckless and cowardly attack, but let me be absolutely clear, our resolve remains firm. I say again, the British government has no selfish or strategic interest in Northern Ireland. But we expect all sides to make peace their single priority. We will work with any political party which signs up to that. We cannot solve the fundamental disagreement overnight, but I believe we can end the violence, and commit to resolve the outstanding issues by negotiation and compromise, on both sides, in place of armed conflict. Once again, to be absolutely clear, we will talk to representatives of Sinn Fein, and to the loyalist parties, when the paramilitary organisations they support have declared a full and permanent ceasefire. We still believe that is possible, and we will continue to work towards it. What I would like to add today, in response to rumours we have seen in the news this week, is that we expect and insist that none of the parties in Northern Ireland, and neither of the two governments, has any contact with paramilitaries, offers them any aid or advantage or succour, as long as their campaign of violence continues. The security situation is the domain of the police and the military only, and they have our full support.'

Up in Derry, the Sinn Fein boy was anxious.

'This thing about no contact. Where does that leave us? I mean, how are we supposed to get anywhere if there's no contact?'

'I wish you wouldn't take him so seriously. This is for public consumption. We get on with what we need to.'

'Here, but he just said the total opposite.'

'Read between the lines. That's the British way. Get on with the job, and don't make a fuss.'

45

Henry was having forty winks, when he heard a hubbub.

Up and out among them.

'What is it?'

'You were right. The gloves are off. London has approved a major operation against this ASU. They're going to try it on, and we'll be waiting. The intel is damn good. If you ask me, PIRA want rid of these bastards too. We're doing their dirty work for them. A mucky deal has been done.'

'You don't mean between us and PIRA?'

'Not in so many words. Thomas à Becket style. Nods and winks. Filling in the blanks. They're learning to speak our language.'

'Who's running the op? Bernard?'

'You won't like it. Polly.'

'Just what I need. Is he here?'

'Flying in from London tonight. Tricky bastard, isn't he?'

'Not my greatest fan. We had a run-in last time. Perhaps he's the forgiving sort.'

'No match for you, I'm sure.'

'Kind of you to say. Let's hope we never find out.'

46

Up at the farm, Pig was in tears.

They all piled in the back kitchen for the squad meeting. Nobody could believe what they were looking at. Sitting in the corner by the range on the wee stool like some old biddy. Crying his eyes out, the cratur. Sobbing and wheezing. Sighing and moaning.

'We're fucked, lads. We're finished. It's over. This is no joke this time, no trick to test your stuff. This is deadly serious. They're back on the roads. They're all over the town. They'll be moving in on us any day. We haven't a chance. We're finished.

'London said they were in earnest about steps towards Irish unity, but that was a fucking joke. And Belfast said they would back us all the way, but they've hung us out to dry. The only reason they sanctioned this squad was to get rid of the lot of us. And all the Brits are in earnest about is sending every one of us home in a coffin, and they're not going to stop until it's done. Youse can all see there's no way we can defeat them militarily. So it's time to throw in the towel. Call it off. Unconditional surrender, and we'll see what comes next. It can't be any worse than this.'

Diamond it was who got up. He had the cowboy boots on him, all his country and western gear, the chest stuck out. The wee fake diamonds on the big belt buckle gleaming and glimmering. It was hard not to stare.

'This here's a squad meeting, and I'm entitled to say my bit. And just so you know, I say nothing behind any man's back, so I'm telling you right out in front of everybody, and you can just cool the beans. That there, what you just said, is a steaming pile of bullshit. You told me the other week I don't have the right stuff for the fight, but that's the one thing you're lacking yourself. The higher-ups put you in charge, but who could listen to you? You surrender if you like, but you'll be on your own.

'Or, I tell you what. Even if all these men surrender, every other squad, the Army Council itself, I won't. If I'm the last man standing, I'll keep the struggle going. I'll be a one-man Irish Republican Army. And do you know why? Because I've read my history, and if I know anything, it's that you don't get a damn thing from the Brits by asking nicely. There's only one language them cunts understand, and I'm just the boy to give it to them. I won't give up fighting until justice is done. History is on our side, boy.'

A couple of the lads actually clapped. But they soon stopped. Old Ned was getting to his feet.

A good minute, minute and a half.

It was like when a chopper went over. You just had to look at your shoes and wait.

Then he was up, and he spoke.

'All well and good, McDaid. You're a fine soldier, and you have a wise noggin for your years. But you're still a young man. I've been around the block a few times. I'd been around the block a few times when you were still in nappies, aye, and when your daddy was still in nappies, so just you listen to me now.

'Go on you young men and make a bit of dinner, and the wiser heads will have a bite to eat and sort the thing out. Between the lot of us we'll decide what's best. That's the way it has to be done, and that's the way it will be done.'

So Diamond and the Other Jack got the stove lit, and filled a pot with water, and they boiled a joint of bacon, and fried up some cabbage and the cold spuds left over from the day before. And they brought it in to the older men, who chewed at it, saying nothing. And when they were done, and every man had had his fill, old Ned spoke up again.

'Pig. Listen here. The start and the end of this thing is with you. What you say goes, no question about that, but I know you want to hear from the rest of us before you call it. So. Listen to me now. I know the right thing to do, and there won't be a better plan than this one. It's been in my head a while now.

'First things first. I don't want to be the man to say I told you so, but I fucking did. I told you not to take Achill's girl off him, but your pride got the better of you, and you went ahead and done it. You shamed that man in front of the whole squad, and he's as good a man as we have. We need him, and that's all there is to it. If the Brits see he's back in action, we'll stop them in their tracks. A few squaddies stretched on the road, and they'll soon change their tune. We just have to work out how. What we can say to him, and give him, to get him back in action, and keep him sweet. Otherwise we really are finished. Twenty-five years of Irish blood and suffering down the jacksie.'

Pig was nodding his head like one of them wee dogs in the back of a car. 'You're right, Ned. You're right. Every word of that is bang on. We've had no luck since he left the squad, and what's worse, he was right what he said, the Brits and the peelers both were scared to come near us while he was around. And just like he said, here I am, crying rivers of tears for him to come back. Wasn't I the fool. Proud and stubborn, just what that man said. God forgive me. I'd near say that man should be leading this squad, not me.

'So here's what we do. I'll give him his woman back. And here's what else. I'll swear an oath in front of everybody that I never laid a finger on her. Yes. And I'll give him my car. And wait till you hear. Wait now till you hear what else. He can take his pick from my sisters. My daughters, even, when they're big enough. On top of that, his pick of hookers, any time he wants, I'll bring them in from Dublin or anywhere, French girls, Swedish girls, whatever he likes, I'll arrange it. The stuff I just ordered for the summer, all his. Decking. Garden furniture. A brand new barbecue, never been used once.

'But that's not the half of it. Wait now till you hear. He can have a cut of my business, the fuel and the livestock both, for the rest of his days, and for his seed and breed after him. And if London agrees to pull out this time round, if we get a united Ireland in my lifetime at all, I swear he'll get his pick of the cushiest jobs going in Dublin. Top salary, beautiful digs, big fat pension, the works. And he won't have to lift a fucking finger. Tell him. Tell him I'll promise him all that.'

'That's the stuff,' says Ned. 'Good man yourself. Right. Waste no time. Mannix, his old teacher, is up visiting and he can go along, with Sid and that Zola Budd fella. Get moving. We haven't a minute to waste.'

47

Sid and Budd and Mannix driv on over to Achill's place. Black night as it was, they found him in the garden with the guitar on his knee, lilting a few old rebel songs. The Broad Black Brimmer and The Men Behind the Wire. Just humming and strumming, but they thought that a good sign.

He was on his feet the minute he saw them. So was Pat.

'There must be something badly wrong if ye two are here. And Mannix as well, if you don't mind. I'll tell you up front, my feelings haven't changed, but the three of ye are welcome. Come on on in.'

He took them in to the good room. Pat got them drinks. He knew what. Stout for Budd, whisky and water for Mannix, and Diet Coke for Sid, who never touched a drop.

'Get a fry going there, Pat.' Pat put rashers on the big pan, long streaky ones, and thick slices of black pudding, and a whole string of the good sausages, and cracked a half dozen eggs in there too. He sprinkled on a few of his herbs, but nobody minded. When it was ready, he served it out onto plates he had warming in the oven, and Achill brought it in to the men. Pat followed behind with a pot of tea and a plate of toast, the red and brown sauce. They all got stuck in.

After they finished, Sid spoke up. 'That was a great feed altogether. You'd get no better at Pig's place, for all his bragging and blowing. But listen now till I tell you.

'We're fucked, Achill. That's the message I was sent here to bring you. They have us beat. The SAS are on the job, just waiting to pile in. They'll make out like we were about to launch an attack, and every one of us will get a bullet to the back of the head. London knows what's going on. Belfast winks the eye. It's all done on orders direct from the top. The Brits don't want peace. They want victory. Surprise surprise.

'There's only one man can save us. You know what I'm saying. You, Achill. You're the only man can dig us out of this hole. You were right, the Brits are shit-scared of you. They know what you're capable of. They know what you've done in the past. You're the only one they fear. So here we are, begging you to come back and join us. That's it, plain and simple. If you can swallow your fury, wait till I tell you what Pig has in store for you.

'No! Listen to me a minute, and then you can say your bit. Please. For me. Just listen.

'First thing, you get your woman back. And here's what else. He'll swear an oath in front of everybody that he never laid a finger on her. Plus he'll give you his car. And wait till you hear what else. You can take your pick from his sisters. His daughters, even, when they're big enough. On top of that, your pick of hookers, any time you want. He'll bring them in from Dublin or anywhere, French girls, Swedish girls, any kind you like, he'll arrange it. The stuff he just ordered for the summer, all yours. Decking. Garden furniture. A brand-new barbecue, never been used once.

'But that's not the half of it. Wait now till you hear. You can have a cut of his business, the fuel and the livestock both, for the rest of your days, and for your seed and breed after you. And if London agrees to pull out, if we get a united Ireland while we're all still going strong, he swears you'll get your pick of the cushiest jobs going in Dublin. Top salary, beautiful digs, big fat pension, the works. And you won't have to lift a finger. He'll promise you all that.

'But lookit. If you can't get past your fury, and your hate for Pig, then I can respect that. But for fuck sake, do it for us. For the ordinary volunteers, who look up to you so much. You're like a god to the young ones. Like a fucking film star. You could be the one who brings back an SAS scalp. Or half a dozen. The poncy Brit bastards in there think there's nobody among us who's their equal. Nobody who can match the fucking Who Dares Wins. Show them all they're wrong. Show them what the Irish are made of.'

The rest of them nodded, and looked to Achill, finishing his tea. He got his wind up, and wiped his mouth. He said his piece there and then, no messing about. The words came flying out of him.

'I'm not going to waste your time chit-chatting. I hate nothing more than a man who won't tell you what he thinks to your face, so I'll give you just what's in my head, nothing more, nothing less.

'Nobody can change my mind. The armed struggle is going nowhere. The man who jukes out of sight, and the man who fronts up every time, they both get treated as bad as each other in this here squad. And they both get the same reward at the end of it. Each one's as dead as the next.

'Let me tell you something. I've thought nothing for myself this last nine years. More. Like a mammy bird feeding crumbs to skinnies in the nest and going hungry herself. I gave up sleep, and saw friends killed, and got wounded myself, all for the sake of the pride of these men here, these Northern men.

'But listen to what I'm going to tell you now. Here's a question I never heard asked. What difference who runs a country, if people are looked after and free to get on with their business? What fucking difference? And then here I am among this unit, fighting for Pig's brother's pride, because the wife ran off. What the fuck am I at?

'I've said it before. Ye all heard me. I planned and executed operations that have left Pig looking like the best OC there ever was. He gets the glory, and when I take out a security van or a cash machine, I hand the lot over to Pig. And I know he keeps the half of it, or more than the half, then shares out half of what's left among the men, and sends the rest up the chain. And he knows I know. I told him to his face, you all heard me. But I ask no questions. Things are done the way they're done. And right enough, he gave what he gave to us, each man got his share. I asked no more.

'But then, out of all of us, and including the bastards who've done nothing for him, and including even the cunts who've schemed to bring him down, out of all the volunteers in this brigade, he comes to me, who's done nothing this nine years only on his orders and for his glory, and he takes my precious wee girl off me. And away she goes.

'Well fuck them both, is what I say. They deserve each other.

'But tell me this, Sid. Here's the real question. Why have the Irish to fight the Brits? Answer me that. Why is there any Provisional IRA at all, any Óglaigh na hÉireann? Because we love this country? Because Dog loves his woman? And is he the only man who does? Don't the unionists and the loyalists love their country too? Don't the Brits? Every decent man does. Every decent man loves his woman too, and I was no different. I fucking loved that wee girl, for all she might have wanted only glory from being round me. So he can't fool me. He can't fool me. I know him too well.

'And damn sure he needs a bit of help now. While I was with you, the Brits never dared send the SAS in. Them boys stayed where they knew the ground, they hardly left the barracks, except when there was a quick job to do, in out. I faced them before, and I tell you this, they were lucky to get away in one piece. Now it's a different game.

'So I tell you this too, one final time. I won't be taking on any Brit. Do you hear me? Them days are done. Not today, not tomorrow, not any time. I'm in the car and back home to my da in Castlebar. And wait till I tell you now. There'll be a welcome there. Oh, there'll be a welcome there all right. Big Achill O'Brien will be waiting with open arms for his son and heir. For I've done my bit. No man can say I haven't done my bit.

'And wait till I tell you what else. I have plenty of cars and women and fucking brand-new barbecues waiting for me in Castlebar too. You tell him that, in front of them all, so they know what kind of an OC they have, in case he'd try the like again. You tell him all that. And he wouldn't even come and ask me to my face, the cunt.

'The hell with him. The hell with his dirty bribes. He isn't worth the steam off my piss. He could offer me ten times every penny he has, twenty times. He could offer to make me the richest man in Ireland. He could show me a car and a woman and a bag of notes for every blade of grass on his farm, in this whole fucking country, and he wouldn't change my mind. Not until I see him suffer what I'm suffering.

'His daughters? I wouldn't take them if they were Cindy Crawford. If they were Marilyn Monroe. There's plenty of fine women for me in Castlebar. Through the whole of the county Mayo. I could have my pick, if I wanted. I've had offers. I can have had a nice comfortable life, working with my da, any time I want. There for the taking.

'Listen now to what I'm going to tell you.

'There's no pockets in a shroud. Do you hear me? You can be as rich as Croesus, and lose every red cent, or have it took off you, and you can always make it back again, if you're smart, or just go out and take it, if you're a hard man. But once you lose your life, you can't get that back. You hear me? You can't get that back. I'll say it one more time. You can't get it back.

'I've always known that if I stayed with the Ra, sooner

or later it would be the end of me. I've known it from the day I took the oath. But I stuck with it, for I knew I'd be remembered for what I'd done. I'd be a legend for what I'd done.

'But lately I've had a bit of time to think, and now I can see there's another side to that story. I don't have to stay. I can go home, and live a long comfortable life. Do you see what I'm saying? Nobody will know or care who the fuck I am, but I'll die of old age, the way a man should, surrounded by his family, and his wealth, in his own home place. And right now, at this time of life, that suits me just fine.

'Death looks like glory to a young man. Get a few more years on you, and glory starts looking a lot like death. And I've seen a lot of death, and it's nothing to write home about. Blood and bones and shite. It took that man Pig to wake me up to it. So I thank him for that. For showing me the truth of what I thought I was about. The great fool I was, fighting another man's fight.

'And here's the last thing I have to say to you. I advise ye all to give serious consideration to doing the same. Away on back home. Forget the whole thing. There's no path to a united Ireland that I can see, not in our lifetimes. There just isn't. I wish it wasn't true, but only a fool would tell you the reverse. The South doesn't want it, and they won't push for it. The Brits don't want it, and even if they did, the unionists won't allow it.

'So London's made up its mind. And that means the fight is over. Tell the boys I said that. If they want to kill

Brits out of revenge, or for the fun of it, or just to get their picture in the paper, go on ahead. But don't think for one second they're achieving any political aim. If you want a good plan of action, it should be to steal away and live in peace among your own people, keep your head down and your mouth shut and make the most of what you have.

'And forget about attacking that base. I'll tell you that for nothing. Without me, ye are fucked. Mincemeat and bone meal. Ye'll be scraped off the road with a shovel. But I think you know that already, Sid boy, or you wouldn't be here.

'Mannix, if you want a lift back to Castlebar, you can stay the night here. We're hitting the road first thing in the morning.'

'Where you go, I go,' says Mannix. 'Your da tasked me with two jobs. Stick by you, and teach you what's right and what's wrong, and I'm not going to give up now. If I haven't managed that second, I can at least carry on with the first. You could offer to spin me back forty years, and I'd say no. But just let me tell you this.

'I ran away from a quarrel too, when I was a young man. It was a dirty business, but listen now and you might learn something.

'My da was a terrible man. Couldn't be kept on the lead at all. And this one time, he was riding a wee girl who worked in the golf club. It's true. And I'm not proud of this, but my ma was awful annoyed, and she begged me to steal the girl off him, to take her to bed myself so she'd see the oul fella for what he was.

'And I did. I was young, I knew no better. And the da got wind of it. He cursed me up and down, swearing that no child of mine would ever sit on his knee. And I was that upset, near I came to putting a bullet in his skull. But killing your da is a fearful crime, and I thought I'd take off instead. The family locked me up, fearing I'd run, but I got away. Out the window. Take more than them to hold me.

'I came to Castlebar, and your da took me in and trusted me with your education, for he wouldn't have you in any school about. I taught you everything you know that didn't come from Big Achill himself, from when you were two year old. You sat on my knee when I fed you bits of dinner, aye, and many's the time you boked it back up all over my good shirt. And it was hard for me them times, knowing that no child of my own would ever sit on his grandfather's knee.

'Everybody loses the head sometimes. But it needn't be a one-way street. If you're a praying man still, pray hard, to St Joseph, and the Blessed Virgin, and St Anthony. They won't fail you. But if you refuse to ask, they can't do a thing.

'I tell you this. If Pig himself was still cursing you, I wouldn't offer to change your mind. But he's a different man. If you seen him. Weeping for you, just like you said he would. He's sent the best of his men here to beg you. To beg you.

'The divil a one blamed you for doing what you did. We all know the kind Pig is. But if you listen to the old stories, nobody hangs on to their fury for ever. If you're a Christian at all, you have to find it in your heart to forgive, at the end of the day. Look at all the films, the good old cowboy pictures. It's the same story. No man who lives by hate and anger comes to a good end. At the heel of the hunt, every-body sees the light. There's still time to change your mind. You'll be a hero to these men yet.'

Achill looked awful tired.

'Were you not listening? A hero is the last thing I want to be. I'm finished with all that playacting. Come on and stay the night here. We'll decide what to do in the morning.'

'Come on away out of this,' says Budd to Sid. 'Achill can fuck himself. He doesn't care a damn for us. He doesn't care a damn for Ireland. He's as bad as a tout. Worse, for touting at least takes balls.'

They could see the rage shaking him, but he kept it in. He stopped at the door, but, and he spoke to Achill now, right to his face, jabbing his finger, snapping his teeth.

'I'll say this to you. If I kill a man's brother, or his father, or his child, and they didn't deserve it, I'll find the money to look after the family left behind. You will too. Or the Ra itself will. Even the Brits do the same thing. For that's the only way we can all go on living with each other. You have to right the wrongs you done.

'And that's what it's all about at the end of the day. That's the only thing it was ever about. Justice. And when justice is done, you have to leave the wrong behind. You have to. Nobody wants to live in fury their whole life. Sure we're only fighting in the first place to get beyond all of them wrongs, to get back to the peaceful life we deserve, minding our own business, running our own affairs. We have to keep our eyes on that. Otherwise the streets of this land would be heaped thick with blood and guts, if every hurt was avenged by an equal hurt, or a greater. It would never stop.

'But here you are, refusing to back down for the sake of a wee slut you've known a few weeks! Did you not hear the man? You can have any girl you want! Come on, Achill, for fuck sake! Wise up, would you?'

The blood was up now. The passion flowing through him. No better man.

'You won't fight for pride, is it? Then you're no man! What else are we fighting for, if it's not pride? Anybody who wants to keep his head down and get on with his life is welcome to go ahead. But not us, boy. We're the men who stand up and fight! Fight for what's right! It's our pride as Irishmen that makes us fight! Our sacred right to self-determination! We won't take the humiliation of another nation ruling ours, no matter who they are! If you want to call that pride, fine, it's pride! But whatever you call it, there's no better reason to fight!'

The air was humming with his words. All eyes on Achill.

'I can't argue with any of that,' says Achill. 'But any time I think of his big fat face, the fury is back in my heart. The way I know I'm a man is that I couldn't look Pig Campbell in the eye without putting my fist through his teeth. He's the one who treated me like as if I was a child. A woman. Treated me like pure shite.

'But tell him this. If the SAS or the Brits come after me myself, here or anywhere, they'll know what's what. I'll fight them if they threaten what's mine, don't you worry about that. But until that day, ye're on your own. And that's all there is to it. Go on now, and tell him all that.'

48

Back they went to Pig.

'Come on, then. What's the story? Is he coming back, or will his pride not let him?'

'He's as full of fury as ever he was,' says Sid. 'He might head back to Castlebar in the morning, he says. And he says he'd advise every man here to lay down his arms, and head back to his home place too. He says there'll be no united Ireland in our lifetimes, and there's no glory in dying for an empty cause. Mannix stayed with him, in case he wants a lift back.'

They were stunned, every one of them. Nobody was expecting that. Nobody knew what to say now. The thing was hopeless.

Maybe not every one. Diamond spoke up. 'Pig. I wish to God you'd never sent these men on their knees, for all it'll do is swell the head. He's going to be worse now than ever he was. The pride will be blooming and bursting in his chest. But let him be. He'll go or he'll stay. He'll come back when he needs to come back. And if he doesn't, then fuck him.

'Listen now to me. It's my turn to say what's what. We get some food into us, and a good night's sleep, so we're ready for tomorrow. And the minute the sun's up, we get ourselves in order, to fight the fucking Brits. We get a plan of action together to take them cunts on. Otherwise we may go home in shame. That's the only thing we're doing here. That's the beginning and the end of it.'

They all went to bed that night happier men than they had any right to be.

49

Back at the Ships, Ned was in full flow. He'd seen the like before, many's and many's the time. He'd heard all the pros and cons for and the pros and cons against, but there was only one way to deal with this sort of thing that he knew. They had to do what the Brits themselves had done. Hunker down and defend themselves. Close the border, is the bottom line. Dig out the big potholes, so no car can get by. Dump hardcore on the wee back lane. Take up the cattle grids on the other lanes, so none could pass except over the wee bridge, which they'd have well watched. Slow them down. There was story after story of the Brits drifting over the border accidentally-on-purpose and whoops what do you know, stumbling upon a squad who just happened to be passing. Take no chances. Give them no excuse.

And then pick our moment, and hit them hard. Start right now. Get things in motion tonight. The squib was ready, all the groundwork was done, it was just a question of getting the wheels turning, and choosing a day. Sid had been working on this one for years. Him and Diamond would do the come-on. They were to drive past in the van, then drop the back door and shoot out from behind the armour plating. Then high-tail it out of there. That would bring a few of them out, and Budd would start to roll the horsebox forward. A thousand pounds of nitrate, with a Semtex booster. Bang. Carnage. And Achill was to target the survivors. That was always the plan. But Pig himself would step in there. No better man.

Then back to the Ships and just dare them to come and get us.

The day was picked. The job was on.

50

The night before, Pig had a funny old dream. An oul woman came down and stood on the roof of the Ships, and she screamed at them all to get up and fight, this was the day they would live or die, and it was theirs for the taking. She was the oul woman you'd see in them drawings and paintings about the Celts and the druids. The woman in the long dress who was always crying at a grave.

He woke up feeling a thousand per cent. Blood pumping. Like he was seventeen and ready to head out on a float, nothing planned, just driving around looking for any old Brit to take a pop at. Those were the fucking days.

Well, them days were back. Here they all were, with a shooting gallery of Brits ready waiting, and the job all set. What were they about, if it wasn't taking on the enemy? Diamond was right. You might as well go home if you weren't going to fight. Take the war to them bastards. Remind them what they were up against.

He got his gear together. The necklace he was given by the ANC boys when they were over to visit, hard wee square beads, black and green and yellow, strung on a whang. The scapular the Basques left behind, that he kissed every time he stepped out the door. The wee skull ring he was given by the header from Farc, when he came over to observe their training, and give a few tips himself.

Two Armalites in the boot of the car, that he'd had customised. A guitar strap on one, with the word Whitesnake and the big curly snake, that he'd bought off the lad with the ponytail at the guitar shop in Armagh. Damn it, that boy could play.

Pig loved looking at the snake. It was strong. It was evil. It didn't give a fuck.

He dug it out from the clatter of loose tapes by the bed, put it on the stereo. Here I Go Again. That was the stuff. He wanted to bang the old head, but he hadn't the hair for it these days. He whacked it up full for the chorus all the same. A good oul tune always gave you the shove you needed. He'd made up his mind. He wasn't wasting no more time.

And a brace of shorts in his jeans, stuck behind the belt at the back. A couple of spare clips under the seat. Properly tooled up.

He drove out to the top of the Danann Fort, round where there was the wee car park. The rest of them were all met again. They sat there, the engines ticking over. Nobody spoke. Just smoked a Regal or sat looking out over the country. Their own country. They were taking it back today, or they would die trying. That's what it felt like. They all knew that generations of men had done the same. Sat or stood or ran or rode horses on this same ground, over them same fields, fighting thon same enemy. Some of them were the very same families, and he was willing to bet some of the Brits were too. Bad blood.

One day it would be over. One day the last fight would start. Why not today?

And on that day, he knew, he knew with no shadow of a doubt, they would win. When that fight was done, they would be free at last. And if it wasn't this time, then when that blessed day did come, his name would be spoke out among the list of heroes. Robert Emmet. Wolfe Tone. Charles Stewart Parnell. Padraig Pearse. Michael Collins. Dan Breen. Bobby Sands. Shane Campbell. Those men fought hard for the true cause every one, but anybody says they didn't fight as well for their own glory, to be remembered as heroes, had never lifted a weapon in anger. That was what drove you to the line. Otherwise you'd let somebody else do it. But no.

And Pig had done more than most. If he sat quiet and listened, he could near hear the glory pumping through his veins. When you started, they always told you the average was a year before you got plugged, or arrested, or had to flit. Not him. He thought of every kill he had his name on. Five of them, plus the Brit that Dog caught that time. More than most. In between there'd been loads of others they'd got ready that they didn't go ahead with, or called off at the last minute, or sat outside the man's house and then just didn't feel right about it, like as if somebody was watching them, too many strange faces hanging around, and so they packed up and went home. Probably a hundred jobs they discussed, and twenty they planned, and half a dozen got ready to go, for every one that went ahead. And out of those, some were hits and plenty were misses. Of all the operations they set in motion, you were lucky if one out of fifty made the news. Most people never appreciated it was hard fucking work. Tedious. Frustrating. Soul-destroying.

The first was a UDR reservist. Easy pickings, but it kept the pressure on and drove the wedge in, for the outrage on the ground stopped the moderates getting too cosy with each other. Pig had been doing bits and pieces since he was fourteen, but that time his da asked him did he want to get his hands dirty, and he said he did. His da said Tubs Kelly would look after him, and he himself would know nothing about it and he didn't want to know. Pig went up to Donegal for training one long weekend. There wasn't much to it. When they got back, Tubs said he was ready. He talked Pig through it a few times, and then said just do exactly what I do. The two of them waited parked in a car at the man's house, for him getting home from work. They saw him pull in and get out. There was a crazy-paving path up to the front door. Pig saw the hall light go on and the front door open and a wee girl's voice shouting out 'Daddy, Daddy! I won!' They got out of the car. Tubs took his short out and held the wrist with the other hand. Pig did same. Tubs called the man's name, and the man looked around. Tubs emptied the bullets into him, six or seven. Pig did the same. The first few when he was standing there, the rest on the ground, right in the face. He saw the skull crack apart and the brains running out. They were getting back in the car when Pig heard screaming coming from the house. Tubs took off and didn't stop till they were over the border. Listening to every news until it was read out. Like the football results. Fist in the air when it was. That made it real, and worth having done.

The next was the same year. A garage man that used to fix vehicles for the police and the army. The statement after was going to say he'd been warned off, and there was a bit of debate before about whether he really had been or not. In the end Pig said it didn't matter, it was well known this carry-on made anyone a legitimate target and he would get what was coming to him. It was the usual drill. They were passed the address, and they had dickers watching him for weeks, getting a feel for his routine. Then Sid went out and did a close study, and timed the whole thing. The man was like clockwork. It was going to be a piece of piss. Big hedges round his house you could hide a cow in. The two of them waited for him to come out. But they were only there about ten minutes when he appeared, far earlier than they were expecting. He stepped out of the house, and they went to move, but at the same time he turned and headed back, like as if he'd forgot something. Pig went to duck back in the hedge but Tubs had jumped on out. They saw the man see them and run inside. They went after him and got him in the living room. As they lined up, he was shouting, 'What did I do? What did I do?' His neck burst open and big holes tore in his chest, pink gristle and white bone. Only when it was on the news did they find out they'd shot the brother of the man they were looking for. Their boy was on his holidays and the brother was going in to feed the cat. He was an insurance man, no connection with anything. They put it out that he was raising money for loyalist paramilitaries, but nobody believed it. It was took as a sectarian killing, and a Catholic in Belfast got shot dead in his taxi two nights later to even the score. Just one of them things.

The next was a few months later. Him and Tubs waited outside a reserve RUC man's house in the morning, when he was heading out. They'd robbed a British Telecom van and dressed up in the gear, with a box of tools open beside them. They were fiddling at the bottom of a phone pole, but Tubs told him not to fuck with anything or they might knock off the phones for the whole town. Pig was looking at the wires, trying to work out what connected to what and how the whole damn thing worked, when he got a dig in the ribs from Tubs. The man was out the front door and walking to his car. Tubs had said Pig could shout the name this time. He was a stickler for that now. He said it kept him up at night worrying he might get the wrong man again. He wasn't a fucking psycho. So Pig stood up and said the name, and your man turned around with a big grin, like as if he was expecting them and they were bringing him a present, and said, 'Yes, gentlemen?' And Pig raised the short and put three in the man's chest. He was waiting for him to fall but he just stood there, pishing blood out of three wee holes. He raised the gun to put another one in the man's face but he looked so surprised and like his feelings were hurt that Pig didn't want to, and so he lowered it and shot him in the bollocks instead. He didn't know why he did that. The man fell then and started screaming, and Tubs came over and put another three in his head.

Hair and teeth and rotten stuff all over the tidy wee lawn. The fucking stink of it. Pig kept feeling like he could smell it off his hands for weeks after. In the car and away.

The next one was a close thing. Pig and this new young lad Devlin were waiting around the corner where this UDR reservist stopped in his van every morning to buy his fags from the wee shop. When he was coming back to the car they driv up alongside. Pig's gun jammed, and the young lad Devlin lost his nerve. Pig grabbed the gun off him but the UDR fella was back in the van and off. Pig jumped out and put what he could through the back window and they saw the van swerve and into the ditch. They drove past and he was twitching away like a dog hit by a car, so Pig put another couple in him and away on. Turned out he'd took the back of his head off with the first shot but it was a chancy thing. After that Pig said he would take a break from pulling the trigger, before somebody else said it to him.

The next one was a squib. He never knew who put it together, but it was delivered to the usual place, and he picked it up all ready in the boot of the car. There'd been a big debate about where to leave it. Drummer McConville was in charge now after Tubs went on the run to the States, and he said that since Enniskillen they had to be extra fucking careful to only get exactly who they were after. That was orders from the very top. In the end it was put in a schoolbag in the hedge, near where they left a massive tanker bomb that was really a dud. The mix had been mixed wrong and it was no good. So they came up with the idea of leaving it near the base to be found and made safe, and then when the soldiers were all congratulating themselves, they'd get a few of them while they did the follow-up search around. That was Sid's idea. Pig was in the top of a house looking over the base. The wee old woman was tied up downstairs. He'd had to smother her wee dog because it wouldn't shut up yapping, and then she wouldn't shut up gurning about the wee dog, so he told Dog to tie her and gag her and promise they'd get her another wee dog when they were done. He had the mobile phone in his hand watching. They were brand new in them days, and it made the whole thing a doddle. He waited till he saw three soldiers go over together, and he pushed the button to dial. He heard it beeping through, and then the ringing tone. And then whoosh. There was no ball of fire like in a film, just a big wind he could feel himself, near put in the window he was watching through, and just for a second he saw the Brits flying back like they were on strings. And it was only a glimpse, but he swore he saw one of them breaking apart as he flew. Literally the arms and legs coming off him and tumbling their own way. He heard later they were finding bits of him in the trees for a week after. Scraping him off the branches before the birds could get at it. Pig was away out the back door and on a motorbike they had waiting. That took them to a garage just up the road where Sid had a car waiting. As long as they drove it nice and slow they'd be grand. Dunging their keks until they were over the border, but loving the buzz at the same time. Stay south for a couple of weeks. All quiet. Job done.

Then Drummer had a heart attack and Pig was put in charge.

Once he was the boss man, he stopped going out on jobs. Stuck to organising. And Achill was right. He'd never taken on the Brits himself, out in the field, man to man. Took a shot at them, and give them as good a chance to get a shot back. He felt that one hard, when he let himself.

Well all that was about to change. Today was the day.

Pat

51

There was a famous story told how the last lot of weapons from the States got into the country, only a few years before. This is a good one. Wait now till you hear.

The whole idea of talks was only starting up in them days and there was a young one on the Dublin team, and she was a real diehard republican, though she kept that to herself. A girleen by the name of June, and she got to be friendly with one of the London boys, a very snappy dresser. Juno and the Paycock, the Dublin crowd used to call the pair of them.

Well. He had a file they were keeping on weapons might be coming in on the sea, sniper rifles from America, heading guess where. The years of evidence, the cases they were building up. And there was a big landing supposed to be due in Donegal. Once he heard the day and the place confirmed, he was to give the nod for an operation to intercept it. They were coming on a freighter, but they would be dropped off the coast and brought in on a dinghy.

But he'd blabbed some of this to her, and give her a wee look at the file, trying to impress, for he had an idea they might become more than friends. And she got a notion in her head that this might be a useful acquaintance to cultivate.

She got him oiled up one night, three sheets to the wind,

and just when the crack was really getting going, she said she had to head on. He wouldn't have it, but she said it was very important. She gave him the quare yarn. Told him she was going to her friends' house to give them a wee bit of relationship advice. The fella won't sleep with her any more, is the thing, and I've been worried about the pair of them. She told me all their secrets, do you see, what she used to make him do, and you would blush listening to it.

Juno gave him a flavour. It was all true, about these friends, but she'd picked her subject well. There's nothing like talking to a man about sex like as if it's nothing to you, to put ideas in his head. He'll get the notion you're a goer, and trying it on. It worked a treat.

No hurry, says he. Your friends can wait. Come on back to my place first.

She was having none of it. Are you out of your mind? What if we're seen? It might look like we're up to something underhand. There'd be outrage. Can you imagine what the papers would say if they got a hold of it?

But she danced around it, and she got him to suggest going back to a wee hotel, a place you'd never know was there unless you knew it was there. Told him to meet her in a couple of hours. In the meantime, she called in to see the friend in question, for Juno wasn't a real goer herself, nothing like it. But the friend got the picture, and showed her a couple of tricks. Told her a few more stories. Lent her some stuff. Juno's jaw was on the floor but she was laughing too. Now she knew just what to do.

A few more drinks in, she handcuffed him to the bed

and teased him till he was ready to pop. In and out of the jacks getting dressed up in wigs and big boots, unpacking sex toys out of her wee bag, and saying all what she was going to do with him, and the whole time she never touched him even the once.

And he did pop, all by himself. Passed out right there. The snores of him.

Away she flit and left him there, still handcuffed. Boys, but half the country was going mad trying to find the lad, and while they were all running around like headless chickens, he missed the word from his contact, and the stuff was landed and carried ashore. Job done. Delighted with herself.

It was weeks later, when he heard about the first of a new kind of sniper attack from half a mile away, that he put the pieces together. And boys, but he went for her.

She swore blind she knew nothing about it. And he told her if that was so, she could put him in touch with the loyalists. And she did, to prove a point, and talk about evening up the score. Don't fucking ask.

Nowadays, the two of them were in the talks still, a bit higher up than in them days. But times had changed, and when they heard the same American connection might be getting active again, they had the same thought together. The both of them got on the blower to each other and agreed to join forces. They pulled whatever strings they had with Washington, and begged them to clamp down hard on any new attempt to bring in stuff from the sea. The wind was blowing the other way.

Washington agreed, but they said they would send an observer. They wanted to be part of this one way or the other. London wasn't getting all the glory. If there was a good-news story on the way, they wanted their fingerprints on it. Handshakes for the cameras. Keep the Irish lobby onside. An election coming up. Everybody wins.

52

Achill heard the commotion and peeped out the window. He watched a while.

'Pat! Come here!'

'Did you call me?'

'Aye. The state of this. Something's after happening.'

'It looks bad all right.'

'It's just exactly what I said. They'll be back again begging me to fight, wait to you see. You'll have a queue of them at the door, on their fucking knees. But, here. I just saw Ned's car go by, and there was a wounded man in the back, I could hear him roaring. I'd swear it was Macken. Go on round to Ned's place, will you, the new house, and tell me who it is. And straight back here after.'

53

Ned's house was a lovely gaff. You'd never know to look at him, in the oul anorak. But his young one bought all the latest stuff. She always had a gang of fellas in with ladders and buckets redecorating some room or other. The bedroom got an awful lot of attention.

She'd made a gorgeous big feed for Ned and Macken, served it on the good china, and poured them out a dram. They washed, hot towels rubbing off the worst of it. Burned the overalls and gloves before she did anything else, and the towels with them. Swept up the ash every bit and flushed it down the bog. She knew the drill.

And then Pat was at the door.

'Will you have a drop of tea?'

'I daren't stop. Achill sent me, and you know the temper he has on him. He just wanted to know who it was got hurt, but I can see for myself it's Macken. I better go and tell him quick. I daren't cross him.'

'He has some fucking nerve,' says Ned. 'That man has no notion of misery. Does he not know the lot of them, nearly, are lying wounded? Diamond, Sid, Pig himself. Achill's a good soldier but he has no business pretending he cares what happens the rest of us now. Is he waiting till the Ships itself is in flames and us all lying dead in the road? Some fucking nerve. Wait now till I tell you.

'The job was going like clockwork. All until Budd let the horsebox go, and it crashed on the gate and just sat there. That was supposed to take the front off the place, and bring swarms of them out like headless chickens. Pig was to take Achill's part, up on the hill, and pick off as many as he could. He'd be happy with nothing less than double figures. Another Narrow Water, to put in the scales against Dog's woman, so he could hold his head high again around the country.

'But the Semtex never went. I'd say they'd been at the stuff in the dump. Do you get me? They were waiting on us. SAS, the works. It was a set-up, a fucking ambush.

'But Pig took a shot anyhow, and that was it. They opened up on us then, and they must have been firing five minutes solid. Pig himself was first to get hit. Right in the elbow. Nothing too bad, but boys if you'd heard him squealing. You'd have thought he was having a baby. The Other Jack got him away. The peelers took their time. The Brits kept their distance. Too fucking quiet if you ask me. But we took our chances to get clear.

'Diamond was hit too and hiding out, and Macken on his way in to fix him up took a knock from a plain clothes Brit car, left him lying there. We got the pair of them out, and Macken wound up with me. And then Sid was stuck hiding out in the ditch, three or four hours more, before we found him. He'd scraped the meat right off his ribs with a corner of old corrugated tin was in among the brambles. If you'd seen it. Must have been pure agony.

'Only Budd got away clean. The team was togging out for the match found him hiding in the changing rooms. And fair play to them, they got a strip on him and in the game. A patrol went right past and he kept hunched over the hurley stick so they didn't see the height of him. He even put a few over the bar, for good measure.

'Now the boys are gathering, for the Brits will be combing the country and watching the way to the Ships. I've to get Macken up and out of here before they knock on my door. A bad day, no doubt about it, but I may tell you, I've seen worse. Far worse. I mind one time we were smuggling cattle over the border, oh, this is donkey's years ago.'

'Sorry Ned. It sounds like a class story, honest to God, but I have to get back to Achill.'

And Ned lost the rag altogether.

'Fucking sit down there, you ignorant wee brat, before I hit you a skelp. Have you forgot the day I came first, myself and Sid, and we asked you and Achill to be part of this here operation? We'd been stood down for months, since the cessation first come in. The two of youse were raring for it, you and Achill both. And the parish priest was in the house, do you mind that? He told you to keep the big man on the straight and narrow, be a wise voice in his ear. But you're not doing it. Why don't you try and work on him? You know better than anybody how to get round him. I've seen you do it.

'But if he won't budge, then for Christ's sake, get you out there now yourself at least, in his car maybe, with his own hood and coat on you, so the Brits will think he's afoot, and pull back, and our lads will get a bit of a boost, and maybe buy us an hour or two. Do fucking something. That's all we need to get ourselves together, and back across the border. The word around that he's out and about again. It would give a lift to the whole country around. You're fresh and these boys are flattened, you might even chance a shot back at them. Get a bit of glory for yourself.'

54

Henry should have been happy. The op was a success, officially. They foiled the attack, but the end result was frustration. On paper, it wasn't an ambush. It was an arrest operation, an observe and react. But everyone knew the ASU were supposed to end up dead. And every one of them was still alive, so far as he could tell. Soon they'd be back in the South, well out of reach. No time to waste.

Polly and Henry took their cars right up to the border. But they saw what damage was done by Ned and the boys. The pothole in the road dug out so you couldn't get past it. It was thick woods on either side. The vehicles were useless.

The pair of them stared at the map. Henry spoke first. 'Well, suppose we cross on foot.'

'If we could guarantee a quick in-out, that's one thing. But if anything happens, and we're caught over there, that's a major diplomatic incident. We could end up in a cell in Dundalk, on trial even. It's happened before. Ash, in eighty-seven. He drove across into an ambush right by the Ships.'

'You've convinced me. I say it's a goer. Scout the pub, see what's what. Dig in if we have to. All we've got to do is rattle their cage, coax them back across the border and we can get a clean kill. Then if it goes tits-up, we're in the clear.'

Polly shook his head, rummaged in his kit.

'We can't. I'll show you. Give me a minute.'

Henry waited. Stripped his weapon, cleaned and oiled it again. No chances.

Polly panted back to his side, all eager.

'Okay, look. I've had them crunch the numbers again up at Science. Aerial recon says we mustn't. There's a thirty-five per cent chance of success under these conditions, by mapping the results of previous operations onto the available facts of today. Pooh-pooh it if you want. I know you think I'm a technocrat, and full of shit.'

'Perfectly put. I go by my gut, and that's never going to change. I don't give a rat's fart what some Whitehall computer says my chances are. I know this ground, and I know these players, and I say the day is ours. Fight hard for Queen and country, that's the only computer forecast you need in my book. Don't look so panicked, Polly. You have nothing to fear from any fighting, for I don't think you know how. Turn tail if you want to turn tail, but don't be surprised if you get a bullet in the back.'

'Are you threatening me?'

'Certainly not. But since you bring it up, it's worth pointing out you'd never know whose weapon it came from. Mine, as you know, is untraceable by the local plods.'

'I'm afraid I'll have to call it in if you take one step over the border. Direct order from London. We don't take them on. Wait for them to make the next move.'

'Since when do you receive direct orders from London?'

'Not everyone is what they seem, Henry, even on our side. Back to base. Right now.'

55

Henry had his own strings to pull. He knew how to goad them out. Take the fight to the enemy. If he couldn't cross himself, he knew who could.

He put in a call to a local politician of his acquaintance, that very same cousin of Crisis Cunningham's, a well-known local individual by the name of Mr Paul Bright.

Mr Bright knew just what was called for. He suggested locally that the army could certainly tolerate a show of support from those loyal to the Crown in the neighbouring villages. An Orange Hall had been burned the last month, and the people still felt very bitter about it.

A few more calls were made, words had in the right ears. Up they came, a few of them even wearing sashes and bowlers. Mr Paul Bright himself among them, in a thick black coat, black leather gloves, wee woolly hat. Near looked like he was going out on a job himself. Henry could see known UVF among their numbers too. Off-duty RUC, UDR reservists. And a few of the ordinary decent Protestant folk of the area, who would only stand up to be counted at times of greatest need, when their patience had altogether gone. Quite fed up of walking around this part of the world apologising for their faith and their culture, wondering who was peeping at you and why, feeling like you had a target on your back every time you stepped out the door. Worth turning the tables, once in a while.

Ned was sent word they were on their way up. He knew what this meant. The border sealed. The hammer was coming for them. Bash bash bash. No quarter given. And he knew nothing to do only get down on his two knees and say the rosary. So that's what he did.

'Hail, Holy Queen, Mother of Mercy, hail our life, our sweetness and our hope. To thee do we cry, poor banished children of Eve. To thee do we send up our sighs, mourning, and weeping in this valley of tears. Turn then, most gracious advocate, thine eyes of mercy towards us, and after this, our exile, show unto us the blessed fruit of thy womb, Jesus. Oh clement, oh loving, oh sweet Virgin Mary. Pray for us, oh Holy Mother of God, that we may be made worthy of the promises of Christ.'

When he was done, it was time to get Macken in the car and away out of this. See if he could get the length of Donegal. But before he could get his coat on, he saw Sid's car outside. Sid himself, Diamond, and Pig. They all stepped out, limping and holding other up. It was a sorry sight.

Pig was ranting the minute he was through the door.

'What are youse pair doing hiding down here? The SAS wants to break us, and leave the Ships itself in flames, and it looks like they're well on their way. I hear that big ginger one said he wouldn't go back to the barracks till every one of us was plugged. I thought Achill was the only man who'd turned his back on me, but it looks like every one of the squad has, this whole country, since you've all let the Brits get in round us. Months of work on this job, years, down the fucking toilet. And why? Here's why. Touts. Touts everywhere. One of youse could be the next, for all I know.'

Ned stepped in between Pig and the rest, before somebody swung at him.

'Take her handy, there, Pig. Things will happen the way they happen. It's just the way it is. They have their day, and we have ours. The Brits have crossed the border before, and nobody's stopped them. Some dirty deal done, that's plain. We have to accept the word of the higher-ups. We don't run this war. We can't change where it's going.

'But wounded men can't fight. We need to sit nice and calm, see if we can come up with a plan of action. It's no good wasting volunteers or munitions on pointless operations. Our people are running about the place all through-other. Nobody knows if they're coming or going. Sit down here beside me till we think this one through.'

Pig sank down in the chair. The wind had gone out of his sails. He looked twice his age. He looked like his own da, is what he looked like. The big long face on him.

'Operations? Operations is the last thing I'm thinking about. Not this time. It's finished, Ned. Admit it. London's turned its back on us, and Dublin, and now Belfast too. Away we go across the border, and back on the run. Dundalk is where we need to be, and stay there. I'll send word to the Army Council that I support an unconditional ceasefire and immediate decommissioning. There's no shame in saying you're beat when you're beat. When the other man has you on the floor, you raise the white flag and talk terms, you don't keep plugging away till he locks you up, or puts you in a box.'

Well, if you'd seen the scowl on Sid. Talk about looking daggers. The words came flying out of him.

'What sort of putrid shite is crawling out from behind your teeth, Pig Campbell? I wish to God you were OC in some fancy bit of Belfast or Derry, where you could pose about and get slaps on the back down the town, and not sitting here claiming command of these hard fighting men. Do you know what I'm going to tell you now? You don't deserve the volunteers you have under you. They have the struggle in their blood, diehards to a man. You deserve a crowd of cowards to command.

'All we've been through, and you want to throw in the towel? You're going to tell the country and the world that the last thirty years of bloodshed was all for nothing? Hold your tongue, in case word of this gets out. Such drivel as no man in your position should ever let out of his bake. Are you doting, or what is it? I'll say it to your face, Pig, and I can't believe I am saying it, only it's the God's honest truth. You don't know what the fuck you're talking about. And worst of it is, that it's taken me till now to see it.

'You seriously think the rest of the movement will hold together when they hear tell you've run off to Dundalk? There'll be chaos, through the whole of the North. They'd all be lifted, half the membership. We'd end up extradited and hung out to dry, no question.'

Pig was quiet. Nodding the head very small. Not like himself at all.

'It hits me hard to hear that from you, Sid. Them's very harsh words, and I take them to heart. Fair enough, then. I'll make no man turn tail against his will. On condition one of youse comes up with a better plan. I'm all ears.'

Ned it was who spoke. 'Let's just wait and see what happens. There might be a wee surprise waiting on all of us. I have a feeling the Brits could end up back in their base the night. We'll know soon enough. In the meantime, we may lie low. Switch on that TV and see is there anything yet. It's a quare few years since I seen my ugly mug on the news.'

56

Achill saw Pat coming, and he let out a laugh.

'What ails you at all, snivelling and crying tears like a wee girl grabbing at her mammy for to pick her up and carry her? Have you had bad news that I don't know about? If it was my da was dead, I'd have heard before you. Or is it all too much for you, seeing that shower of cunts get their medicine, shot and lifted and battered by the Brits like they deserve?'

Pat gave a big sigh out, like as if it was his last breath.

'Jesus, Achill. I hope to God I never feel the force of the blood fury that you're showing this day. Yes, it's too much for me. Do you not hear what's happened? The job was a total disaster. Half the squad are lying wounded. Men who've gone years, aye, and decades, without a scratch, now bleeding their guts out. Diamond. Sid. Pig himself. You won't fight for their pride, but you'll sit here from your own pride and let others suffer, men who never done a thing on you. And now all are saying there's an Orange mob on the way up to burn the Ships. Are you made of stone? At least drive out and lure the Brits away. Make them send the men who are battering your comrades to follow on after you instead.

'But if you won't, then at least let me go out myself and

put some heart back into the country. If I'm seen about in your own car, with your own coat and your own hood, the Brits might think it's you back on the scene and ease off for the night, and then they'd have a chance.'

The poor bastard. If he knew what he was doing, asking that.

'I have no secrets from you,' says Achill, 'or at least not the kind you're talking about. If you knew the pain I was suffering. It hurts my heart to see that cunt Pig rob a man he's no better than, in broad daylight in front of everybody, just because of his rank. He took that girl away from me like as if I was a foreign national sniffing round the local talent.

'But I was never going to stay as angry for the rest of my days. On you go. I did say I'd fight again when they were in my own country, and if they're going to take the Ships, then that's bad news. If Pig had just had the decency to deal straight with me, then I'd soon fill the ditch with half a dozen dead Brits.

'But you know well I can refuse you nothing. And maybe I can find a shred of glory in that stupid fucking plan. Go on then and do what you said, and draw them away. As soon as you have, mind, get yourself straight back here. Take no chances. Don't get involved and go sniffing for glory. You're not a fighting man, and nobody thinks any the less of you for that. And if you make a fool of yourself, it's my reputation that'll suffer. Let them do their own dirty work.

'Ah, Pat. If it was up to me, the Brits and the Ra would

kill every man of each other this day, and just you and me left to step into the ruins of that base. Then I'd die happy. Fuck the lot of them, every last man on both sides.'

57

Pat took Achill's own hood, that no other man had ever worn, and pulled it down over his face. He put his arms through the body armour, the thin light stuff Achill had paid a fortune for when they were over training in Libya, watching go-go dancers and drinking fake whisky with Gaddafi's boyos. Pat had heard all the stories. Then the blue anorak over it, that had the red stripe down the side, the one every man around knew to be Achill's. He'd wear nothing else. Only his weapon Pat didn't take, the famous M90, for it was too much for any of them bar Achill himself.

Then Achill took out the beads that Theresa had give him one time, and knelt, and said a decade of the rosary, like he hadn't done this ten years or more.

He prayed that Pat drew the mob away from the Ships, and sent the Brits back into the base like he wanted. And he prayed that Pat would come safe back to him.

Of them two things, only one came true.

58

Pat waited till he heard it for sure, then he drove straight up to the Ships.

He saw the Orange mob, the off-duty peelers leading them, ready with petrol and rags to burn the place. He saw flames already leaping at the windows.

The tummy was jumping and the hands were shaking, but no point thinking about it. He let a few rounds go over the heads of the ringleaders, and if you'd seen them lep and scatter like sheep in front of a hungry hound. That calmed him down.

The word went round fast who it was, for they knew the colours. The sniper himself. He was back. Pat near believed it himself. The whole crowd tripped and tumbled their way down the wee lane, and across the border.

Pat let out a wee yelp. He had driv them out of his land, and back to the country they called their own. He wasn't stopping there. No way. On he'd come, to drive them beyond again.

Pat had the stirring in his breast, roused up by his own heroics. For a second, he got a glimpse of what it must be Achill felt.

He liked it well. You don't listen to what a man says. You watch what he does, and you know who he is.

This was who he was going to be.

He was shaking, but he was buzzing as well. Straight on down into the town. Hid down behind the big bins at the supermarket. The crowd was gathering again, but none of them saw a hint of him. He was doing like he thought Achill would, lining up a shot at the big gate of the base, waiting for one to come out. He was the sniper the night.

The gate swung back and he saw a white car. Was that the same he had heard Achill talk about? He poked his head up to check.

Full in the face he got a two-by-four, and it took him back a foot, lying there flat, the hood tore off him, the head spinning three different ways. He couldn't make out the man standing over him. Black coat, black gloves, wee woolly hat. The rest of the mob piled on in now, beating at him with sticks and bats, hammers and bottles.

They were scattered when they saw a peeler coming. Forbes, a fearless young buck. He'd been waiting on this all his life.

He raised his revolver and Pat tried to stand, bleeding and hobbling.

'Hands in the air!'

But sure, Pat's arms were broke. And Forbes knew that well.

'In the air! Or I'll have to shoot!'

He was near laughing. Oh fuck yes. He squeezed the trigger, and one tiny lump of lead and steel at a thousand mile an hour whacked into Pat and floored him over again. Just delighted with himself. A taste of your own.

'I'll take it from here, officer.'

Forbes turned. Henry, looking like he meant business.

'Secure the area. No onlookers.'

Forbes didn't argue the point. He put away his gun, did what he was bid.

The body armour had saved him, but Pat was in and out of himself, still dizzy and leaking blood. He tried to focus. Who was this now, coming to plague him more?

Henry loomed over huge, like a bird hovering. The words came flying out of him.

'You fucking idiot. Don't move. Don't fucking move. Where are the others? Or were you stupid enough to think you could take on this base solo? Where's your fine friend O'Brien? Didn't he come to your rescue? Fucking coward. Are you out here on his orders? Don't come back without the scalp of that SAS captain? Well, you met your match tonight.'

Pat managed a wee smile, a last croak up at him.

'Aren't you the big fella, pointing your gun and threatening a man already half-dead? I could have took on three of you. It was them fucking Prods, and that fucking peeler, who brought me down, and now you walk in to kill me a third time and claim the glory. Well I'll tell you this. Achill is coming for you the night. You can't escape him. Count the hours.'

Henry reached down and unclipped the armour at the bottom, by the belt. Pat wriggled but he could do fuck all. Henry aimed his weapon square at Pat's guts, three inches away, and pumped lead into him, bang bang bang bang. The man lay dead at his feet like a bag.

Henry crouched, and spoke nice and soft to the quiet face.

'My fate isn't yours to dole out, young man. If he comes, I'll be ready, and may the best man win.'

59

Dog saw Pat bite the dust. The big one left him lying there and legged it through the cordon, back to the base.

Fuck.

But Dog knew what was next. Evidence tampering, a cover-up. He'd seen the whole thing before. He wasn't letting the Brits get to that there body. He knew just what they'd do. Hoik it into the car and burn the lot, destroy every shred of evidence, to thwart the inquest. Come up with a yarn about the petrol tank catching. Nobody would question a word of it. They'd done that number on Minty Morrison. Not this time, bucko.

Dog had a wee dander down that direction. Hung around away from the cordon. And there waiting on him was young Forbes, who'd put the first bullet in Pat.

'Clear off, Campbell. This area has been sealed. Police investigation.'

'Listen, cunty-hole. I seen the whole thing. Your cards are marked now. If you know what's good for you, get to fuck. Did you ever know Ivor McDonald? I don't think he had last Christmas with his dear wife and loving parents, so I don't. A spare plate of turkey and ham that year. I can arrange the same again. I've seen off far better men than you.'

'I know well you have. Officers from my station, friends

of mine, good Ulstermen doing their duty. And maybe now's my chance to even up the score. It might brighten up next Christmas for those families if I could send word I'd got one back.'

'Bring it on. Try your luck. I think we both know how that story turns out. You, then your wife, then your da, then your kids. They'll all go on the list. Let it take ten years, they'd be got every one, some way or other. If I was you, I'd disappear for half an hour. Have a wee patrol round the other end of the town. I hear there are a few suspicious-looking characters hanging about. Leave me to get on with what I need to, and we'll say no more about it.'

That saw him off.

Dog stepped back again to the shadows. There could be a chopper down any time. He knew he was caught if he went near the body, but he was afraid he couldn't hold his head high in the squad if he left Pat to rot there on the road.

He stepped to the phone box, gave Budd a wee tinkle.

'Can you meet me at the back of the handball courts? Bad news.'

Budd was there in ten minutes. Dog filled him in, what they had to do.

'We need to get the body back to Achill, for the SAS are on their way down to burn the evidence. They'll want to hush this one up, and I'm fucked if I'm going to let them.'

Dog was ready to move, but Budd held him.

'Whisht. There he is. That same hallion, with the red hair. I'd know him anywhere.'

'What is he at, anyway? Tampering, I was right. He wants to get the forensics cleaned up. The brass neck on him, right in the middle of the town.'

'Either that, or he wants him dumped naked in the road, the way we do it. A warning.'

'Two against one? I say we take him. Are you carrying?'

'Aye. Come on to fuck. We might not make it back, but I have that feeling.'

'Me as well,' says Dog. 'But if you're right, then this here's the way I'd rather go. And if we do make it, I'll try and get word to Achill, and you hold the fort. We can't let him down, Budd. Pat was the kindest, gentlest man I ever knew.'

60

Henry pulled the hood and jumper and jacket off the body. O'Brien's clothes. He crunched the cloth in his hands, and wondered what stories it could tell. He saw the body armour under. Quality. Lighter and tougher than MOD issue. I'm having that. He unclipped it.

He scanned the perimeter. No one.

Wait. There.

He saw the two of them coming, Brian Campbell and Hughes. He saw what was in their hands. He saw in front of him what it would lead to. Another corpse. His own blood on the road.

His wife.

His son.

He told himself this was the right thing. He'd got what he came for. He didn't want any complications. He could have taken them, easily, but one death to answer for was quite enough. That's what he told himself.

Back in the car, and back to base.

61

Henry was braced for the earful in the ops room. He wasn't disappointed.

Polly was in the chair. He was purple with the fury.

'What the fuck was that display?'

'He was a clear threat. I'll account for everything.'

'I don't mean the kill, you moron. The kill is the only decent thing you've done this week. I mean running back here. Were you trying out for Brands Hatch?'

'It was a tactical retreat.'

'It was a funk. You let yourself be scared shitless by two bogtrotters. You could have taken them on, made it a clean hat-trick. You know what happens now? The RUC will refuse to patrol, the green army won't dare go out. If they see the SAS retreat from those men, what chance do you think we have of locking down the town?'

'You've got some nerve, calling me a coward. I thought you had a little more between your ears. You don't know what the field is like until you're out there. You make the judgement you make in the moment.'

Polly let out a big sigh. He gave Henry a sad wee smile.

'I've been putting it off, but it's time to break it to you. Face it, Henry. Your best days are behind you. Don't feel bad, the time comes, that's all. I'll get you a training post in Hereford. Or you can take on something in the private sector, start investing for the school fees. No, listen. I understand. No hard feelings. You need to accept who you are now. You've done your duty, and it's time to pass the baton. Things are changing here. We have a different approach these days. The word coming from London is kid gloves on the ground. The real work is done on another level. Sneaking around in the field has had its day.'

Who you are now. Something twisted in him there. He felt it rise up. He would show them. Polly, Anna, Bernard, London, fucking PIRA. All of them.

'My duty? My duty is to take those bastards on.'

'I'll sign you off.'

'Don't you fucking dare. I'm going back out tonight, and just try to stop me.'

'I'm signing you off, Henry.'

'I'm sorry, with all the gunfire this morning my hearing is a little below par just now.'

'Stay right where you are. That's an order, captain.'

'Try to stop me, and see what happens. Just see what happens.'

'I said, that's an order. Direct from London.'

62

On down the road, Dog passed Anthony Rice, Ned's youngest fella.

'Good man Anthony. I need you to do a wee message for me.'

'Just say the word, fella.'

'It's no small thing. It's not been give out yet, but the SAS got Pat.'

'Took him in?'

'Took him out. Emptied him. The whole thing is a massive fuck-up. But that's where we're at. So run on down to Achill and tell him. He knows nothing.'

The face on Anthony. White as a sheet.

'If you're not up to it, don't be afraid to say. No bother at all.'

'I'll go, course I'll go. But, Jesus, Dog.'

'I know. I know.'

'What's going to happen?'

'Let me tell you a thing, Anthony. You can never tell what's going to happen. You just can't. All you can do is what you have to, and then wait and see. But you have to stay on the front foot. The only way to fuck up is to do nothing. That's all I know anyway.'

63

That poor bastard Achill. When he saw Anthony coming, and the face of him, he half knew the score. He'd heard the town centre was sealed off because of an ongoing incident. He couldn't help thinking the worst. But maybe it was all right. Aye, maybe it was nothing at all.

Anthony knew better than to try and put a spin on it, or do anything other than say the plain truth.

'I'm awful sorry, Achill.'

'Is it Pat?'

'It is.'

'Is he dead?'

'He is. I'm awful sorry, Achill.'

Achill nodded. He kept nodding. He looked small. He looked shaky.

'Aye, I kind of knew it when I seen you coming. I kind of knew it when I got out of bed this morning. The first time I lay eyes on that good young man I kind of knew it. Whatever my hand touches turns to ash. The fault is my own. Tell me what happened.'

'I seen nothing myself. Dog it was sent me down. He says he watched the whole thing, and it was the SAS. They stripped him and left him in the road, and then ran for the hills when they seen Dog and Budd coming. Them two are with him now, keeping dick, waiting till it's clear to bring him back up here.'

64

When the body came up, Achill roared out his grief.

Anthony held him by the two hands, for he was afraid Achill might take the carving knife and do himself an injury. He was thrashing and bucking on the bed. All his anguish, for his country, his friends, himself, came rioting out.

The whole street and half the town came by weeping, for everybody loved Pat. The place was soon a wake.

And in the door with some of the first came Achill's old friend Theresa. She'd heard when she was having her hair done, a few other women with her. A terrible business. They all said it. That man has no luck at all. Poor Achill. Poor Pat.

She sat down by Achill and put her hand on his.

'If you take them on, you're sure to end up the same way.'

'I might as well be dead, for I couldn't protect that gentle boy.'

'You can't save everybody.'

'But I'm not trying to, Theresa. I never understood myself till this minute what it was I was even fighting for. All this time I've been saying I wouldn't fight another man's fight, but it's for the ones not able to fight themselves that I should be standing up. The trigger men are all going to hell, no doubt about it, Brits and Ra both. But my job is to protect the innocents, adults and children alike, the ones that don't have the strength to protect themselves.'

'You saw where your fury led the last time. This time might be worse.'

'No, Theresa. I go now to end that murderer, but not for him. For his country. To show them evil doesn't go unpunished, that there's consequences to taking the innocence of a quiet wee land and trampling it down. They need to feel the pain we do. They need to see what it is they've done, know it in their guts and in their blood. They've called it upon themselves. Ireland, free or not, was never the point for me. Budd was right, what he said. It's about justice. If they're let think that it's right to rob the freedom and the dignity of another people, that we accept them as our betters just because they say they are, then we surrender any claim to self-determination. If we don't fight, then we admit we have nothing worth fighting for. And they showed us how. We fight how they fight. Hard, and dirty. No mercy. So the men they put up to stand in our way have to die. Simple as that.'

Everybody tugged at his cuff, everybody had a word of comfort to try to ease his heart. But he cared nothing for them. Even Big Sheila, the local Shinner, tough as old boots, she wasn't shy of coming round him and bending his ear, and he hadn't the heart to chase her. He had no heart for anything.

'The thing is, Achill, we need answers. Hard proof this was cold-blooded murder, and then we can get that proof to the papers and the TV, and that'll blow their position out of the water. They say they want peace, and they're provoking us back to war. It'll give us the strongest hand we've had since Bobby Sands. What do you say?'

'I won't go naked to them. They have my body armour, my gear, my hood.'

'Leave that to me,' says Theresa. 'I'm owed one more favour. I'll be back by morning with the kit you need.'

But Big Sheila wouldn't let it go. 'If you can show your face some way, Achill. Just to let them know you're about. To put the fear of God back in them murdering bastards.'

'Spray it down the town, on every gable end. Get them Sniper at Work signs up again. Cover the town in that there message, so it's all they see when the cold sun is up.'

It was done the way he said. The signs went up on poles, red triangles round the black silhouette of a man with his fist punching the air, hood on his head, rifle in the other hand. Sniper at Work sprayed on every wall and road. The word was out.

But Achill wouldn't leave the body be. He trailed along beside it, sat there while they washed it and got it ready. But he said plain there was to be no proper wake, and definitely no funeral, until he brought an SAS man's bones back here, to show to Pat.

'You'll not go in the ground before one of them is meat on the slab. That's a promise. If it's the death of me, them cold-blooded cunts will suffer what I have. God forgive me, I lied to your poor oul da when I said I'd keep you safe. My own death is coming fast, but not till I even the score.'

65

In the base, the Brits took stock. The printers were chattering away, the phones ringing non-stop, the fax machine squeezing out reams of stuff. Reports and memos, charts and graphs, photos and diagrams.

In the ops room, Polly was at the board, looking very sombre.

'You've all seen it. The message is quite clear. He's back on the scene. Our informers say the same. And that changes things quite dramatically. If previous experience is any guide, then as soon as we appear on the roads, he'll take his revenge. We can't keep the media away from that. The end of our hopes for another ceasefire. The leadership in Belfast will have to embrace his actions, for fear of splitting the movement, and then the talks are dead in the water. It'll put us back ten years at least. I'd prefer to avoid that particular blot on my copybook. So we return to the status quo. There's no way he'll take us on solo, it would be madness. We wait it out. Our priority is not to lose a single man, not to provoke the slightest contact, and let the talks proceed. We're part of a bigger picture, we must forget the local politics.'

Henry was pacing, fretting. It wasn't right. It fucking stank.

'Let them win, in other words.'

'Nonsense. Step back from the situation. Show the restraint and maturity we claim to represent in this scenario. Lead by example. Today's death can be part of an internal republican feud, let's say. One of our agents in the community will supply some suggestive graffiti in return. I'll feed something juicy to Fleet Street. And it stokes up the sense that they're weak and divided, which plays into our hands.'

'This isn't an information operation, Polly.'

'Henry, when will you learn that everything is an information operation. Everything. Hearts and minds, remember. Our mission in the world is just what it always has been. To civilise. To moderate. To find consensus. And the only way to do it is by example.'

'You seriously think if we play nice, they will?'

'Perhaps. But there are hearts and minds on both sides. Our country needs heroes just as much as they do. That's where you come in, Henry. We have you marked down. The perfect poster boy. Your name will be a byword for old-fashioned British pluck, if I have my way. That's our plan of action. You take the hearts, I'll take the minds.'

'Listen, Polly, just listen. I can take him on right now, before dark. Bring him in. Show him he can't strut around making threats.'

'Absolutely not. We take defensive positions against the intel of an attack from O'Brien. Give him absolutely no excuse, so if he's stupid enough to try something, we have the moral high ground.'

'Polly, we already have the moral high ground! We are the moral high ground!'

'Not to the wider world.'

'Then the wider world can kiss my arse!'

'The wider world is what you're defending, Henry. We don't get to pick and choose.'

'If you want your hero, then I'll step up. Bring him in, dead or alive. I have a duty not to be cowed by them. We have the law on our side. If we back down today, we might as well abandon the unionists and pull out tomorrow. The principle is the same. Defend your people. Show them who's in charge. Engage the enemy, or surrender and go home.'

'It seems you've made up your mind.'

'Just give me twenty-four hours, and I'll give you something juicy for the papers. I'll give you British pluck. I'll show the wider world who the real heroes are.'

'I'm taking a dreadful risk.'

'About bloody time. Just give me my head, this once. I won't let you down.'

'I know you won't, Henry.'

66

The stars were blinking down that night. And if you could swap places, and watch the green country from high up there among them, then you'd see the lights from the Brits there in the base, and more in the next town, and more again, twinkling in a chain across the whole of the border, so many that you'd think you were looking at the night sky itself all over again.

It was a different town after dark. You'd near think the place itself was snoozing, but few enough were at peace. Though it has to be said, the most of the town had no clear idea of what was happening. And nobody beyond that part of the world had any notion at all.

And they never would. For it's very easy to keep a lid on things if you really want to. There was far too much at stake in the talks for a wee skirmish to bring it all down. The Three Monkeys was the word. Besides, most in the place took no real interest, beyond what they saw on the news, and damn sure this never made the news. Oh, there'd be something at the tail end of the bulletin, reports of shots being fired in a certain area, but that was so much blah blah blah to these people. You wouldn't even take it in, let alone wonder what it was.

And it wasn't that the reporters were in on it, or very

few of them. No, there was very little leaning went on, though the odd thing would have to be spiked. It was the papers themselves, the higher-ups in the TV and radio. They lived here too, and they all wanted the ceasefire back in place. Good for business, good for families, gives everybody a nice warm glow, spend their money, keep the ads coming in. They were quite happy to tune out a bit of inconvenient unpleasantness, as long as it was down the country and out of the way. Nothing was ever said. Nothing needed to be. Wink wink nudge nudge say no more.

Achill

67

Sunday morning, first light. An orange sky hanging over the green country.

Theresa found Achill in the chair with his arms wrapped around Pat.

'Son, this one's gone. Take what I give you. It's all there.'

She left a full bag on the ground.

He shook his head.

'The flies are round him already. I can't leave him to rot.'

'I'm bringing him to the undertaker myself. They'll clean him up lovely, do what they do to keep him looking like himself. And when you're back, you can say a proper goodbye. For now, you have to square things with Pig. Come on, for there's no way round it.'

68

Achill strode out of the town, up towards the Ships. If you'd seen the crowd that watched him. Every man, woman and child ducked out to catch him going by. Ones the age of Ned who hadn't stirred from their beds this years cracked open a door or a window, and shouted out Good man Achill, and he'd nod to acknowledge each, without once taking his eyes off the road ahead.

The lounge was packed out. Hanging off the walls. Nobody was missing this.

Sid and Diamond came in and settled, both on crutches. That quieted the hubbub. Then Pig himself limped down the stairs. Dead silence.

Achill was waiting. A different man, they all said. He looked older, is what it was. Calmer, too. Ready.

Had he thought about what he would say, or did he just let it come out? You wouldn't know with the same fella. But out it did come.

'Till the day I die, I'll never understand how Pig and myself came to this over a woman. I wish to God she'd got the first bullet in her back, rather than any of you men come to harm. The Brits themselves couldn't have stitched us up better.

'But I'm not here to stir the pot. I say we leave all that

in the past. It's not right to hold a grudge your whole life, so my fury's at an end. It's the Brits that need to be quaking now. All I want to do is kill, and I'm ready to start right this minute.'

That was the best thing ever they heard. The heart came back into that squad there and then. The place warmed up again. The old team was back.

Pig didn't stand, but all hushed to hear.

'*A chairde*. You listened well there. It's not right to interrupt a man when he's saying his piece, for even a great speechifier might stumble at the like of that. So although I'm talking here to one man alone, the rest of you pay close heed.

'And I know well what youse have all been saying about me, blaming me for this whole disaster. But I tell you now, straight out, it's not my fault. No way. The situation was what it was, and I did what I had to do, given the conditions as I saw them at the time. If I could have seen where it would lead, well. That's another story. And if I was hoodwinked, then I wasn't the first. Mick Collins himself was tricked by the Brits. Our Lord was conned by Judas. There was that famous story about the old king, I just can't think of the details now this second. And even when the SAS were up sniffing around this place where they have no business, still the same notion wouldn't leave me alone. You do what you have to do at the time, and that's all there is to it.

'But since that's the way it happened, and I'm the one it happened to, then I'm the one is going to make it right.

'Achill, here I give to you everything Sid told you was yours when he came down to your place the other day. And plenty more besides. If you can spare a wee minute, I'll bring out some of the other stuff and you can have a look. Boys, wait till you see.'

They all shifted about. Not too sure where this one was going. Please God not another barney with this pair.

'Do whatever you need to do,' says Achill. 'Bring out the stuff or hang on to it, whatever suits yourself, for I'm not going to delay. This whole townland and the green country beyond will know this day the Border Sniper is back in action.'

There was the quare stirring at that word, but Sid raised his hand. All knew he never took the trouble unless there was good reason, and it would be worth hearing, so they shushed again to listen.

'This is going to be no fast wee job, and these men need a bite to eat first. Nobody can take on the Brits without a full stomach. You start stumbling around, you can't think straight, you lose the rag at the slightest thing. But a man with a good feed in him will keep his focus and his strength all day. Let's get some grub on the go, and Pig can bring out the stuff he has for you, so everybody can see. And I don't mind reminding him, he said he would swear in front of all that he never took advantage of the wee girl, and I know that's something you want to hear. Achill, away you go and eat inside in Pig's place, so you don't feel hard done by in any way. We need to clear the air completely. Pig, I hope you don't mind me saying this whole shambles should be a lesson to you, to treat other men the way you'd want to be treated yourself. There's no shame in the boss man holding up his hands and admitting he's wrong, when he was the one that started it.'

Pig was happy enough with that.

'A good spake, Sid. Not one word out of place. Achill, just you sit your ground till I do this. It won't take five minutes. And the rest of you, wait to see this stuff. You won't believe your eyes. You yourself, Sid, go and get a couple of the young lads to bring it all up here. Time enough to start plotting and scheming after our dinner.'

But Achill was having none of it. The words came flying out of him.

'Time enough for bringing out presents and swearing oaths when we have a minute's peace, and I don't feel so fired up. There's one good man lying cut up and cold, that the SAS brought down, and ye want to fill your bellies! If I was in charge, we would get cracking on with the job and earn our feed, once we have something to be proud of behind us. Until then, I'm not swallowing a bite. That poor boy is lying dead in my front room, the whole crowd in there weeping and wailing, and it's far from my mind is eating and drinking. Blood and pain and the moans of dying Brits is where my head is at.'

But Sid kept on.

'Achill, listen here. You're a better man by far with a weapon, there's no doubt of that. But you wouldn't claim to be my equal in wits, even only for that I'm your elder by a good couple of years. So just hear me out. One man, no matter who, can't stop the whole thing in its tracks. Good men die day in day out, and the ones that are left have to bury them, and get on with life. And fighting is our life. We have to keep our own selves in shape, so that we can better get justice for the martyrs to our cause, and make sure they didn't die in vain. We need only one call. All or nothing. We keep it together, as a squad, as a group, as a country. No more going off doing our own thing.'

And that was that.

Up from Pig's place came a new motor, and the garden stuff, never used once, and then a string of young ones you'd blush to see, three of them, near half the age of Pig, bold as brass and giving the men the glad eye, for he'd ruined them completely.

Then Brigid herself. She gave Achill a good squeeze and he gave the same back. And Sid himself brought in the cash, sat it out in fat bundles on the table, and every man leaned in to get a good eyeful.

And when the food was brought out, heaps of pink rashers and strings of sausages, a whole black pudding in fat slices, potato bread golden and steaming, white-and-yellow eggs swimming in lovely clear grease, Pig lifted up his glass.

'A bit of whisht now. Listen up. I swear, by almighty God and his Blessed Mother and all the angels and saints, that not a hand did I lay on that wee girl, may I be struck down if that's any word of a lie. As for the others, I'm saying nothing. But they're all yours even so. Just watch out for the wee redhead. Fuck me, she can go. Keep a bag of frozen peas handy, is my advice.'

The boys gave a laugh, and the same girl gave them the eye and shut them back up again. Which made the other girls laugh. But Achill couldn't stick it.

'Circumstances being what they are, this is the way things have to be done. We sound like fucking politicians. God forgive the lot of us. He's shown what he thinks of us and our doings, and the higher-ups have as well. And it's no more than we deserve. If we're the cream of the crop, this country is finished. Now get that grub into ye fast so we can get to work.'

Away off he went to ready himself.

69

Brigid was brought down to Achill's place after him, but when the poor wee girl saw the sight of Pat stretched there in the coffin, she fell on the corpse and roared and cried, till the make-up was all smeared and the new dress stained and tore.

'God, Pat. Lovely, lovely Pat. You were the best of them here. Last time I seen you, you were sitting smiling in that chair, and now look at you. I have no luck at all. My uncle was killed by the UDR, my two brothers dead on the roads in the one year, but you never let me cry about it. You told me the best was up ahead, for I'd be the wife of this man Achill, and he'd take me back to his country and the wedding would be the last word. You'd organise it all yourself. Sure the times we used to sit and pick out flowers and dresses and trousseaus and table favours and the whole thing. I'll never forget you, Pat. You were the kindest man I ever knew. I hope you're at peace, wherever you are.'

Every man in the place tried to get Achill to take a bite, they begged him, they would have shoved it down his gullet if they could, but he only snarled at them.

'If any man will listen to a word I say, would you give over about eating and drinking. I have no stomach for it, and I won't take a thing until sundown, when all this is finished.'

In the end, he cleared the place out. Only Sid, Pig and Dog, Ned and Mannix stayed behind, to try and calm the head. But nothing would do him until he could get at the Brits.

'It used to be you, Pat, laying out the food on the table, and fussing and footering at your wee biscuits and buns, and making sure I had enough in my tummy before I'd go out on a job. The heart of me wants nothing to pass my lips. It wants nothing only you. It wouldn't be worse news if I heard my own father was dead, who's at home there weeping for a son who's risking his life for the sake of some culchie bitch. Nor it wouldn't be as bad if the child of mine I hardly know, over there in Scotland, was dying or dead. Before this, I wanted nothing only for me to die here, fighting the good fight, and you to go and bring that boy back to Castlebar, Pat, and let him hear the man his father was. I used to lie in bed dreaming of that, over and over, and it gladdened my heart. Isn't that a funny thing to be thinking? Fathers and sons, Pat. I wonder now is my old da still going at all, with the worry he must have over me. The whole thing is a terrible business when you stop and think about it. God forgive me, Pat, but I'd sign away the republic itself if I could have you back here to watch me do this today. You'd have some wee remark would make it all seem okay. God forgive me bringing you anywhere near it all. I'd happily offer up my own life to bring your smiling face back. I'd offer up the lives of every man here. We've done plenty to deserve a bullet in the heart. You never done a thing. God forgive me.'

And it would be a lie to say there was a dry eye among the rest of the men.

But they knew what he needed. They made a hot strong pot of tea, and they got some of that into him. And a wee morsel of speed mixed in with it, to make sure the feet didn't let him down when he got going. Sid took care of that.

70

Achill got his gear together.

He strapped on the new body armour Theresa had brought him, snug against his chest. The latest thing, straight from the States. He cleaned and oiled his weapons, checked them and checked them again. He pulled on the good warm coat she'd brought, and thick army trousers. Last of all, the new hood she knitted herself, down over his head. Tight and warm, clinging to him. Just the eyes showing.

Them eyes. Jesus.

Back behind the wheel of the car, and he felt so fucking focussed, he could see and hear and taste everything. He was the centre of it all. The world was turning around him. He could reach out his hand and stop it. There. See that. The fucking power in them hands.

And he swore the car itself spoke to him, like some kind of a Knight Rider. I'll take you out, it said, and I'll take you back, but the day is coming soon when I'll not take you home no more, for there's a one-way trip coming up for you, son.

And he laughed.

'Don't I know rightly that day is coming? I've known since the day I joined up that I'm never getting home to my own country. Why else do you think I stayed put here, if I could have been back there now? I would have never made it, nor near. They would have surely caught up with me, one lot or the other. And I plan to die on the front foot. But not today. Please God not today. I'll make the most of what I've got left. The Brits will be sick to their stomach of fighting by the time I'm done with them.'

He revved hard, and off he ripped.

71

Back behind the polished colonnades of Stormont, hardly an hour's drive away, London called all sides together for the last day of the talks. A breakfast meeting, with jugs of fresh-squeezed orange juice, plates of croissants, trays of bacon and sausage and beans, tomatoes and mushrooms and hash browns, and steaming pots of tea and coffee. They all filled their plates and cups, and took their seats.

But this time they were joined by another head. Washington had sent their man, in on the red-eye. He spoke first, loud and slow, the way they do.

'Well, it looks like the damn ceasefire is history.'

'The latest communiqués say their bloody sniper has resurfaced. He might well blow the whole thing open before we're ready.'

'See, I'm focussed on a truth-and-reconciliation process. It's moving forward in South Africa, no reason it can't happen here. Families need closure, the society as a whole needs to move on, and that's never going to happen if everybody has buried secrets. A full amnesty, and get it all out in the open. National therapy is what I'm talking about.'

The others squirmed at the thought. More than a few of them knew where the bodies were buried, and the idea that you'd split open the country itself and show the true rotten horror of it, lying there for all to see, well. That was too much. He was asked to submit a position paper and told it would receive due consideration.

After the breakfast session, being a Sunday, it turned out they had a couple of hours R & R scheduled in before the final session, for anyone who wanted to go to church, or see the city. Nobody did.

But it was a nice enough day, by local standards. No wind, only a few big heavy grey clouds and the sun peeping out between them. They all found themselves pacing the lawn at the back, sharing out fags, chewing the fat. London suggested a game of cricket, but the Dublin crowd turned their noses up. Not exactly inclusive, they grumbled. It's a great international sport, says London. The day Ireland beats Pakistan, we can talk about that, says Dublin. The only thing they could agree on was football. Washington raised his eyebrows, until he realised they meant soccer.

'Oh, we have our own game too,' says Dublin. 'Gaelic. A bit like yours, only without the pads and helmets.'

'Well, aren't you the tough guy.'

Somebody was sent out for a ball, while they all got changed into their gym stuff. Then back outside for a kickabout. Five-a-side was called. Not a word was said, but they all fell in along the obvious lines. They were short on numbers on the side of the greens, but nobody did more than raise an eyebrow when the Shinner who'd been hanging around, waiting for proximity talks later on, dandered up and took his place. Him plus Dublin and the nationalists on one side, and the unionists and loyalists, and police and army reps, on the other. The London man kept out of it.

'I'll referee. These things can spill over. If we're going to be neutral, we have to do it properly. That goes for the situation too, by the way. I expect you'll all do what you need to do, exert what influence you can, to keep this current situation contained. I'll stay out of it, but I won't stand in anyone's way.'

Play was as dirty as you might expect. The DUP lassie was fouled just outside the area by one of the Dublin boys. 'You are so dead,' she grinned at him. She got one past them, made the Shinner who'd stepped into goal dive after it, and get a face full of soil for his trouble. He flung a lump of it at the grinning Whitehall chap on the side, got him right in the goolies. And the rest of them started laughing then as well.

The sun went in and the rain came down, but they played on ahead, churning up the grass into sticky muck. Slipping and sliding and guffawing as they all got smeared in the thick slick mud. Who was the next one that threw a clod of it? Nobody could say for sure. But before long, it was flying like a riot. Splatting each other like custard pies. Dripping off them. Caked in the stuff. You couldn't tell who was who any more. Wrestling other down, bucking and kicking. Shoving wet lumps down each other's keks. Roaring laughing at the same time. And then when the rain stopped, it was time for the showers and get on with the day. Great crack altogether.

Oh, there was the odd bruise, and the odd scratch. These

men played hard. The women did too. But it was worth it. Important to break the ice. Time for a pint first, those who partook. A valuable exercise, all agreed. Let off some steam, and keep focussed. That was the way to do it. Otherwise things might get nasty, and nobody wanted that.

72

Achill sat in his car, watching the barracks. He was zen. He was ready.

He thought about the Brits he'd killed, over nine years. Tiny wee men in the crosshairs, dropping when he squeezed his finger. He knew little enough about them, bar the names on the news after. For some reason those always stuck in his head.

Private Samuel Tilling.

Lance Corporal John Ockendon.

Sergeant Keith Kirby.

Sergeant Trevor Clay.

Captain Miles Kissane.

Corporal Nelson Braganza.

Private John McCloud.

Private Carl Shand.

73

Henry had Special Branch in his ear now, and they called the shots. Stay out of sight. This isn't the moment. Not yet. Let the green army take him on, if he moves. If he doesn't, let him go home. This is a fight for another day.

He told them he was going out.

Special Branch and Polly put their heads together. They came back to Henry. There was one way. The play was simple, but risky. If we're going to take him out, it has to be an unequivocal action from him. But if you act as lure, we can choose our moment, and do it with the minimum of fuss. You line him up, we take him on.

He was willing. Though the story he planned had another ending.

He had read through the files. The same names. Tilling. Ockendon. Kirby. Clay. Kissane. Braganza. McCloud. Shand. He couldn't bear for that man to be walking free.

He got himself ready, in the OP. Achill's own jacket and hood, the Aran jumper belonging to Big Achill, over his fatigues, and his kit on top. The body armour under the lot of it. It was tight on him, and he looked the part. Like a half-Ra half-Brit, stalking the land.

74

Achill had had enough of waiting. He knew how to kick things off.

He stepped out of the car. The second he did, they opened the gates of the barracks and the few soldiers and RUC left guarding the scene trotted in. That wasn't like them. But he hadn't time to worry what tricks they were playing.

The long was in a fishing case. He could have it out and loaded and on his shoulder in six seconds flat. The only approach to that base that he trusted was underwater, the river that ran along the side. He waded in, and ducked down. That was the way to get past the line of sight. There was one place to get at them, round the back. They opened it twice a day for the wee Filipino to fling out the rubbish. Any minute now.

He surfaced, and there was a face he knew, right in front of him, on top of a body squatting by the water with a rod and line. For a second he thought it was real. Jesus. That was the last thing he needed, to be seeing things.

He remembered it well. A year ago, was it? He came by a spot on down the same stream, a stony shore just like this one, and saw the wee lad fishing.

He spoke to him now, like as if he was there. Playing it out over again.

'Sean Barney. Did I not have you put out?'

'Fuck sake, Achill.'

'Fuck sake, nothing. I said to you, not two year ago, if I see your face back in the six counties, that's the end of it. No second chances. And are you back chopping spuds in the base again? Have you a suicide wish or what is it? No matter, you have to take your medicine either way.'

'Come on, Achill. Wise up. I'm bothering nobody.'

'You're bothering me. When I put somebody out, they stay put out. What happens my reputation if I start making exceptions just because I'm in the middle of something else?'

'Sure, just pretend you never saw me. I'll say nothing. Give us a chance to flit. I'm not even back a fortnight. You had me put out the last time, sure why is this any different? I tried to make a new life, but it didn't suit me. I thought it was water under the bridge, since there was a ceasefire on. This was the only work I could get. I'm begging you. I'm begging you.'

'You're missing the point, Sean Barney. Who the fuck do you think you are, that you get to not die? Do you see? Pat's dead, maybe you heard. I'm going to die myself in this war, and I'm ten times the man you could ever dream of being. And who the fuck are you?'

But Sean Barney had clung to Achill by the legs, crying, begging, begging, begging, giving it the works. His family, his life history, the whole sob story.

No dice. Achill had held him down under the water to muffle the sound, and pressed the short to his head. There was a massive bubble up from the shot. It popped, and the water around was foaming red.

He'd waded in again to weigh the body down. If he was smart, they wouldn't find him for weeks. They might never find him. They still hadn't, so far as he knew. He'd wedged him in under a dozen of breeze blocks, right down the bottom. Most people said the lad had gone back to England. Plenty of them just melt away when they do.

Achill stepped, and he skidded. Fuck. He sank under, and took a wee chunk out of his shoulder. His own red mixed with the rotten old blood of dead Sean Barney.

He found his footing, got his head above the water.

Right ahead of him, he could see the big pipe coming from the reservoir. Water was gushing out of it. Far too much. He lost his footing again. Felt for it with his toes, his heel. He was caught in a wee whirlpool. The sluice into the barracks was taking in the water like billyo. It was sucking him down. Like the river itself was trying to drown him.

He knew the man at the pumping station with his hand on that tap. Ivan McAlpine. A loyal Orange hood, and they'd tried to get him a couple of times. Now the boot was on the other foot. The Brits had set him up. Covered all the angles. Quick phone calls were easy to make, no questions asked. We need a wee thing done the night. Everybody owed everybody something, and if they didn't, they soon would. You know yourself.

Achill was near crying that he might go like this. 'This isn't the death I'm owed, after all I done. God almighty,

I'll do anything if you'll only let me have a soldier's death, even if it's before I get my revenge. If I'm to be killed by the SAS this day, let me go and face it like a man, but I'll not die like this!'

Before he knew what, he was lying on the bank on his back, coughing up dirty water. He saw the face of the local Shinner, Big Sheila. That mighty woman must have waded in and hauled him out.

'Do what you have to do, Achill. Just don't fuck with the talks.'

And she was away.

75

Inside in the mess, the squaddies who'd been out all day were pissed, slumped, heaped, slipping in sick and slops of spilt beer. The music pumped, the disco lights coloured them red and blue and red again. A few jerked around and ground with local girls ferried in through the back gate from friendly farms and towns. The brass turned a blind eye. The men needed a break. Let them drink themselves stupid. Drown your sorrows. Tomorrow you'll be back in the field.

76

Achill saw his man. Was that him? It was the same white car. Sneaky fucker.

Back to Plan A. He skirted the water and hopped back in his own motor, lit off after. Headed up to Pennymount, the Protestant estate.

Hot on his tail. A hand waved out the window, and the car pulled in on the far side of the estate. Achill drew up beside.

It wasn't Henry. Our old friend Mr Paul Bright.

'You dirty cunt.'

'Did you want a word, Mr O'Brien?'

'You've cheated me. That was my one chance to get in there among them. I would have been our Michael Stone. Revenge for the boy. And you've denied me that.'

'I can't say I'm terribly upset.'

'And you know well I daren't touch you. The Top Men deal. You lay off ours, and we lay off yours. If I take the lid off that one we could be in this mess for another generation.'

'That just about sums it up.'

'May you rot in hell when your time comes.'

'Save me a seat. But don't let me hold you up just now.

You'll find your man is ready waiting for you. No need to sneak around. We know what you're about, and we're game. Take him on, with our compliments. And the best of British to both of you.'

77

Henry had stepped out when Achill drove away. Thank you, Mr Bright. I owe you one. He dug himself in away around the side, by the castle ruin, solo, watching for the return. Calm. Centred. Ready.

Bernard was on the radio. He'd heard the plan too late. He blew a gasket. Now he wouldn't leave him alone.

'Don't take him on, Henry. I've lost too many good men, and I can't bear to lose the best I've seen serve under me. Think of the future. You could have a glittering career ahead of you in London. The foreign service, journalism, Parliament if you want. Make a real difference, if you choose to. I have excellent connections in clubland, they'll set you up with a safe seat. The sky's the limit for a man like you.

'But if you take on this player today, you'll be a scratch on a monument, a footnote in a history book, a sticky picture in your widow's purse. There's no glory in this conflict. Maybe for a young man, when you think you can take on the world, but you and I know better. It mustn't happen. Think of what it means, to both sides. If they can take you, they can take all of us. I see it every time I close my eyes. I see them flooding through the gates, climbing the walls, spraying rounds and tossing grenades. You don't know what it is to get to my age, and still know you might be ripped apart in this awful place. An old man shouldn't die like that, torn in pieces for the very dogs we feed at the gate to chew my cock and balls, lap up my running blood. It burns me up.

'Your mother has been on the blower begging us to order you in. She asked me to read this to you, and I will. She says, If ever I comforted you when you cried, if ever I gave you life at my own breast, then please give me some comfort in return, and take him on from behind the walls. If this man gets hold of you, we won't have a chance to mourn. There won't be enough of you left to bury. Spare us that. If you must die, let us say goodbye with honour. Let us have one last look. We need a chance to make our peace with it, so the rest of our lives aren't consumed with grief and madness.'

Henry switched off his comms. Enough. Blame it on a faulty battery. It happens.

His fucking mother. Of all the idiotic things.

He waited, trying to feel ready, like a snake coiled.

His training. His years in the field. Second nature.

It wasn't there.

He'd lost it. Couldn't get it back. Nothing. Nothing.

He was just a tired, aching man, waiting to die.

Oh, Christ. Christ.

In his heart, he had every thought.

Go back. But they'll sneer at me if I go back. Polly will, who urged me to stay in, and I refused. He was right, I should have. I've fucked it, for everyone. Back at base, they'll say I brought him on to attack them, some half-crazed bogtrotter not half the man I am. They'll crucify me.

Could I go unarmed to negotiate with O'Brien? Offer to turn over Campbell's wife, and throw in a pay-off?

I could let him take the base. Yes. Yes. An unprecedented victory. Offer him the weapons, the intel, all of it, anything, as long as they spare my life.

Good God. What am I, trying to chat him up like a girl? If I step out there to talk, he's just as likely to shoot me down in cold blood. I have to take him on. I have no choice.

He saw Achill walking from the car, straight towards him, head down, looking like a mural. He started shaking. He couldn't stop.

Please, Christ, not now.

I can't, I can't.

I can't.

He ran.

Still thinking, what should I do? Should I take him on? Should I retreat?

But his heart had decided. His bones. Already running. This was who he was. No escaping it now.

78

Achill ran too. Ran hard.

Henry followed the path around the castle ruin, Achill on his tail, baying for blood. Their four feet, thumping down on the grass, through the briars, over the two streams, the clumps of white suds from the drains of the base, that Achill remembered crawling up round once when they were trying to see if that could be a way in, the steam coming out from the laundry inside, and he lost touch for a second with the man he was after, up past the soiled black earth where the bakery used to be before it burned down, but no, there he was again. They ran. They ran like the prize was Olympic gold, but the only prize on offer here was Henry's life. Three times around the old walls they ran, like horses flying around the Killinamoy races. Like a dog on a deer, and Achill roared at his ones to stand down when he saw a couple step up ready to get stuck in, that he'd have the fingers off any man who pulled a trigger and robbed him.

And a certain local politician sitting inside in the base, Mr Paul Bright, gave a glance towards his old friend Polly, who shook his head just a tiny amount. Enough. Leave him.

Big Sheila saw them turn the third time. She had an idea

what to do. She ran by as they passed and shouted to Achill that there was more Brits coming. Just like she knew, Achill didn't seem to give a fuck.

But it wasn't for Achill's benefit she said it. It was for Henry's. So he might think there was backup on the way and he'd maybe have a chance, if he stood his ground.

It worked. The blood came pumping back into Henry's limbs when he heard that word.

One of my brothers will fight alongside me.

He stopped, skidded, tumbled, then back on his feet, turned, raised his hands.

'Stop! Stop!'

Panting like fuck, he could hardly get the words out.

Achill stopped, and raised his long.

'Wait! Wait! Listen! Wait!'

Achill waited. Listened. Took in the man before him.

'O'Brien. Listen. I won't run. Not any more. It's time. One of us will kill, one of us will die. But I want to make a pact. Do you understand? With you. Now.'

He bent, let the breath draw in slow. Good. There. Now. He stood again.

'Listen. Whichever is left standing, please, the other must allow the proper authorities to take charge of the scene. To do what they need to do. There must be law, there must be order. I have a family, you have a family. We each deserve whatever we get, I know that, but our families are innocents. My only fear, her only fear, is that I disappear, and they never know. They never have a body to mourn. Don't torment them beyond the deed itself. And I swear I'll do the same. I won't tamper, I won't hide a thing. The full truth will be out in the open for all to see. Do this with honour. Be the man you are.'

'You listen to me now, Brit. Lions and men don't make deals. A wolf and a lamb only ever want the worst for each other. Get ready to pay for the misery you've imposed upon a dozen Irish families. And for my own.'

Henry's voice was strangled in his throat. He yelped out, hating the sound of it.

'Wait! Wait! Listen to me. Please. Please. I respect you. I respect your fight. This is your fight. Me, now, here. I see that. But you've never targeted an innocent man. I've seen your file. You did what you had to do, as a soldier, and walked away. Don't ruin that now. My wife, my child, are not your enemy. Don't torment the innocent. They're not to blame.'

Achill never twitched. He fixed him cold. The words came flying out of him.

'Too fucking bad, Brit. You brought them into this, not me. If you'd stayed in your own country, minding your own business, they'd have nothing to cry about. None of them would. You know how we operate. You call them innocent, but the same blood is on their hands too. You come here in the name of your people, and rain down evil on our people. That makes your whole country black with the same guilt. Ye all cry foul, but you fucking started this fight. Nobody made you come here and take what didn't belong to you. And you could walk away any time you like. But you chose this instead. You can't say you didn't know it was coming. Every soldier knows. Now get ready to die.'

Crouched down now behind a fallen trunk, Achill took a shot.

Henry hit the floor. He listened for the backup. He'd given them enough time.

There was nothing. He was alone.

They'd tricked him. The idiot he was, trusting a voice from nowhere.

But the base must be able to see. They must know. Surely they'll send out a chopper, a support team, like they did for Alex, to whisk him away.

Silence.

No. Oh no, not that.

He saw it now. London. Polly. They were hanging him out to dry. He knew too much. Getting flaky. Dead men tell no tales. A glorious martyr, to pile on the pressure, give them an edge in the talks. A poster boy who couldn't spoil the story.

The fucking spooks, the fucking politicians. Moving the pieces on the board, doling out life or death with a flick of the wrist. Not one of them was in harm's way. Not one of them could ever die this death. He was charged to defend their will, their country's honour, but all he could ever defend was his own life. It wasn't their blood on the road. It never would be. They didn't understand.

No. They understood. They didn't care.

A deal had been done. Men of their word before men of mercy. The long game.

79

Henry knew now. He was going to die.

And peace came on him at last. It was simple. It was clear. The only thing left was Anna and Max. I have to fight, he thought. I have to fight with courage and with honour, so they can hold their heads high. They will know the man I was. I will know.

He threw himself at Achill.

The two men tumbled, wrestling hard.

Hard on the road, knocking the wind out of them. Both scrambled clear.

Achill saw now what Henry had on. His own gear, his old body armour. The stuff he got in Libya nine years ago, that he'd wore on every job he'd done. He knew how strong it was. And he knew exactly where it was weak.

He ran for Henry again, short in his hand now. That was the way. Close in, like Diamond always said. Let him see you. Let him smell you. Tell him why.

The short dug in under the ribs, at the side. The gap on the left, where the strap didn't close right. One shot, that was all.

Henry felt the barrel tight against his gut.

'Listen! Listen! Swear you'll let them take me home. Please.'

Achill was snarling like a beast.

'I wish I was minded to eat you raw, that I had thon animal passion. You deserve no more. Pat deserves no less.'

'The life you lead is the death you deserve,' says Henry. 'They'll treat you how you treat me. Spare me, and spare yourself.'

Achill pulled the trigger.

And that was the end of it.

A single bullet did the job, but one by one the rest of the squad came up, and each put a bullet in him, for what him and the SAS had done to them, to their comrades.

'That's it finished,' says Achill. 'Wait and see now how long do they cling on to our land.'

Achill backed his car up to the body. He popped the boot, and tied the new rope to the tow bar. The other end tight round the legs. Then he untied it, and turned the body face down, tied it again. Nobody could look.

He dragged Henry back down the track to the Ships behind his car. The head bounced off the road. A trail of him all the way there, for the dogs and the birds.

Holland Park. Sunday night.

Max was deep asleep, ready for nursery. Starting half-days, to ease him in. At eighteen months, her mother thought it too soon. Henry thought it not soon enough.

Nobody asked Anna what she thought. She was left to soothe and balance, as best she could. Steer the middle course. Keep the ship afloat.

But tonight was her time. She was on the phone, arguing with the architect. An old schoolfriend of Henry's, who claimed to know just what he liked. How could he know? The arrogance. These people. She knew.

Henry loved his bath. Anna had a thing about drowning, which meant she'd never been able to learn to swim. This house had a crappy old tub she never used, except to stand in for a shower. She had always resisted his moans. Too small, too shabby. It just wasn't a priority, she told him. There was so much else to do first.

But she saw now. This was what he meant when they rowed, as they did now almost every time they were alone together. She was only thinking of herself. She asked of him, no, she demanded of him, that he think of her, and the child, before himself, but she wouldn't do the same in return.

Now she would. Fire with fire. She'd learned that from him.

He always surprised her when he came back on leave, with something up his sleeve. A trip, a meal, a piece of jewellery. Somehow, she never saw it coming. Now it was his turn. She couldn't stop smiling at the thought of his face. His lovely smile. His eyes closed, soaking there for hours. She would show him what it was to be a wife. His wife. Make a real family, at last. All she wanted. All she'd ever wanted.

She hung up the phone, nothing settled. Her eye was starting to flick. A bloody migraine coming on. Could she risk uncorking a fresh bottle? Perhaps not. So much to do tomorrow. She turned on the radio, to drown out her buzzing thoughts.

'The soldier has not yet been named. Sinn Fein disputed the army's account, calling it British propaganda. But a government spokesman said that in spite of this latest atrocity, talks next week will proceed as planned, and hopes for a new ceasefire remain intact.'

She felt the old cold fear she knew too well. But for once, she forced herself to take his good advice. She found she was able to sit on it, breathe through it, step outside her fear, just as he'd always told her. After all, what were the chances? One in ten thousand. Just spare a thought for the poor widow whose turn it was, and get on with your day.

The phone rang. Three times, before she let in the thought.

She couldn't answer it. Stop. Stop.

It clicked through to the answering machine.

Her own voice, droning the message.

She stopped breathing. She didn't deserve to.

She couldn't bear to stand and listen. She grabbed the handset.

'Hello! Hello!'

Silence.

'Hello?'

'Anna? It's Bernard King. I'm sorry to disturb you at home, but I wanted to call you personally, before the MOD does. I'm afraid I have the most dreadful news.'

82

Why was she kneeling? Why couldn't she stand?

She'd fainted? Was that it?

But she hadn't quite. She couldn't. The baby was crying. I'm alone.

No. Max, in my arms. I picked him up, without thinking. My body knew how. Gave him the breast. Tears dripping onto her nipple, trickling on his lips.

It's my fault, Max. It's my fault. I dragged you into this. Your mother is a selfish bitch. Idiot. Idiot. What was I thinking? What was I thinking? I just wanted you to have a happy childhood, with a wonderful father, and now. All your life. Where's your daddy, Max? Isn't he coming to pick you up? Why isn't your daddy at football? Is Daddy going to take me to the park? But I want Daddy to give me my bath. I want Daddy to read me a story. I don't want you, Mummy. I want Daddy. I want my own daddy. I want my daddy back now!

It's my fault. I should burn for this.

83

The boy slept.

She stepped to the wardrobe. His shirts. His beautiful shirts she'd spent years collecting, thousands and thousands of pounds. For him. An immaculate soldier, but a scruff in civvies. She was going to show him. She would make him the man he could be.

None of it mattered. Had it ever mattered? Had anything? She couldn't tell.

She heaped them all up, at the back of the garden. She had dragged them, still on the hangers, over the wet grass and stone. Piled them high.

What now? Light a match? Nothing. Hopeless.

She tried to remember how to do it. Paraffin, and kindling.

She took her time, built it up. Not thinking. Just doing. Her body knew how.

Whoosh. The heat of it. The rage, the fury.

She watched it burn. She watched it all burn.

84

Monday night. Pat's wake.

They all turned up at the Ships in twos and threes, filing in and standing about, balancing a plate of egg sandwiches and a cup of stewed tea. The women were buttering and cutting like the blazes, but nobody was eating. There wasn't much chat either.

Here's why. The coffin was empty.

Achill had set Pat up at the bar, a flat pint in front of him. Slumped down like as if he was having a snooze. Achill sat beside, hand on the shoulder, dead sober, but talking to Pat as though he could hear him.

'I did what I swore I'd do, Pat. The Brit is dog food. He's here, but. I have him in the jacks, dumped in the drain, and he'll be soaked in the piss of every man among us before the night is done. Nothing is too low for that cunt. He'll be minced up the same as Nairac this time tomorrow. Butchered like a nag. I'll feed him to his own dogs. If I could, I'd feed him to his bitch mother, that brought him to this earth to end my joy.'

Sid stepped in with a soft hand on the arm.

Achill jumped, like as if he'd thought he was on his own.

'Come on, now, Achill. You need to get cleaned up.'

'The fuck I will. Not until Pat is in the ground. I'll wear

the blood of his murderer, to show this boy it was me and nobody else. But go on you, open the bar there and let the men drink their fill.'

Nobody stinted, for they all knew somewhere deep down they needed to get stocious drunk so that this madness might seem like the right thing to do.

And that's what they did.

They slapped Pat on the back and told him there was nobody like him. One by one they sat beside him and told him what they'd done these last days and weeks, the whole yarn. Nothing was lost in the telling.

Watching them, Achill felt the ache in his heart ease just a wee bit, to know he had done what he said. And before he knew it, he was sleeping himself, head on the bar, just like Pat. The two of them snoozing away.

In his dream, Achill saw Pat lift his head from the bar, and speak.

'What do you think you're at? Do you not know I'm lying here bound in Purgatory until you put my bones in the sacred earth of my own country, and I can move off to be judged and find my soul's final resting place? Take my hand for the last time. There's no more Pat and Achill, making plans for when peace comes at last. There is no peace waiting for you, nor for me. Our peace is finished with. For I'm dead, restless in hell, and you're soon to follow me. A bloody killer is coming for you. But you know that well. The only thing I ask is that they bury us together. Will you do that?'

'Do you need to ask? But don't say the last time yet. Let

me hold you once now again, and another time after that, the friend of my heart, so I can feel the life beating in your chest, and a wee hint of the living joy I've lost.'

He reached out, but there was nothing, only cold waxy death.

Achill shouted out, and the whole place leapt like a bomb went off. He looked about him, mad in the eyes, wide awake. And he saw the ugly face of a bloody killer coming for him, just like Pat said.

He drew his short and he would have put three rounds in the man's face.

'Achill! Achill, Jesus sake!'

It was the looking glass behind the bar. The bloody face was his own.

85

There was a plait Achill was growing at the back, hanging down over his collar, what they called a rat's tail. He'd swore before he left the west that he wouldn't cut it until he was back living in his own home place. He sliced it off now and threaded it between Pat's hands, where the rosary beads would go.

Achill called for Pig now, though his heart still hated him.

'Do this for me now, and I'll ask you nothing else. Order the stone. Get all ready at the republican plot to bury this man. He never took another life, but place him there as a marker for the days to come, that a man of peace can be honoured as a true Irish patriot. None of us wants to kill. We only do it to bring about the day when no Irishman needs to.'

But the wake was only getting going.

Achill was something more like himself now, for the first time in weeks. The head was getting settled. Still he wouldn't take a drink, and every one that was poured for him, he emptied out the window to run into the soil, and said it was for Pat. The tears never stopped running from his eyes, but his face didn't once crease in a sob, and the odd smile was there, as he watched the antics of the men around him.

For the drink was flowing now.

Oh, the quare crack. The quare stories.

Still Pat was propped at the bar, getting the odd slap on the back, but the tales the men were telling had shifted into a bit of slagging, and who was better at driving the getaway. How fast they could go, how tight on the bend, and which of them would end in the ditch.

Achill got tired listening to it. All the stuff Pig had give him was laid out on the back table, like a wedding, and Achill said the men should shut up their slobbering and settle it right here and right now, and he would give a prize off the table for the winner.

The men were on it like a hoor in a monastery. They needed somewhere to put all the jizz was in them this night.

First the circuit was drew up, and argued over, and drew up again, the two miles past the chapel and back to the Ships, twice around. Four of them were up. Diamond McDaid, Dumbo Lynch, then Anthony, Ned's son, and Dog himself.

Ned stood in close to his boy, whispering tactics.

'You know well how to take a bad corner, I've nothing to teach you there, but your car hasn't the power of the others. So you need to use the head. The man in a powerful motor will take the corner wide, trusting his engine, but with a weaker engine you need to hug in close. The stone up ahead, the Badger's Toe, is where you turn. I want you close enough that you could reach and touch it, but don't scrape the car or you'll slow yourself down and do damage. If you can pass on the inside there, nobody'll catch you.'

All piled outside. Pat was carried out and propped agin the wall. The men gunned the engines and ripped off, leaping over the wee hills and near on two wheels at the bends. Dumbo went in the ditch at the end of the first lap, and gave his face a desperate whack. Diamond skidded off, but he got back on the road and made it up, though he left most of his back tyres on the tarmac. They came to the spot where the road was too narrow to pass, just as Anthony was side by side with Dog, trying to cut him up. 'Fucking maniac!' shouts Dog, and he wasn't joking. Anthony wouldn't hold back, so Dog had to shift down and take the rear.

At the Ships they could see little enough. The Other Jack and Domino were squabbling over who was in the lead, cash passing back and forth in quick wee bets. But Achill knocked heads, and told them to whisht.

Diamond came in first and claimed his prize, with Anthony next, then Dog. Dumbo, who they all knew to be the best driver, walked up the track with a big long face on him, and a lump the size of an egg on his noggin.

Achill felt awful sorry for him.

'Come on here and we'll let you have second pick, for all knows you're better than the men that beat you.'

But Anthony was having none of it.

'Away and shite. I came second, and second pick is me. If you want to give him a prize, do it out of your own pocket, for you have plenty of stuff of your own beyond to give away.'

This time there was no fury in Achill's heart.

'Good man Anthony. You're dead right, fair's fair. I'll sort him out, and here's the keys of my pick-up for you.'

But Dog was raring up now.

'Wise the bap, the lot of you. Anthony, what the fuck was that show? Your oul wreck would never have beat my wheels in a fair race, but you played it dirty. Some of the rest of you speak up, for fuck sake, before I'm accused of being a sore loser. Youse all seen it. Come on here, Anthony, and swear on the Bible that you never meant to pull that trick on me.'

Anthony, fair play to him, shook his hand.

'Dog, nobody would argue that you're not a better man than me, for I haven't the years nor the miles put in. You know yourself the young have hot heads, and do things in the spur of the moment they shouldn't. So I'll let you have the truck, and if there's anything else of mine you want, to make it right, just say the word and it's yours.'

And he threw the keys across to him.

Dog near caught them in his mouth, he was that surprised.

'You're a decent skin, Anthony. Although you pissed me off, you're a level-headed young fella the most of the time, and we'll chalk this one up to experience. All the same, learn your lesson. There's no other man here would have dared try that number on me. But what your family haven't given to the struggle isn't worth talking about, so here's the keys back.'

The grin on Anthony. Dog wasn't finished, but.

'The truck is mine still, officially, and I can take her out

any time I want, right? But I'll let you keep her, and drive
her, so as nobody can say I'm a sore loser.'

And there was one more prize, a lump of cash, that Achill
gave to Ned.

'All know you'd have beat us flat at any sport in your
day, and it's only the years holds you back. So take this,
that you've something to remember this night by.'

'A good spake, Achill, and I thank you. And it's no lie
you tell, for at the Easter Rising commemorations in 1966,
there was a quare lot of sports got up, and mine was the
first hat in the ring for all of them. A few of the men got
up a bit of boxing, and I wiped the floor with all comers.
Throwing too, though I was bested in the horse riding.'

Achill was on his feet again.

'I won't have it said that we didn't honour Pat with the
same as any of the greatest martyrs of our cause, so come
on then and we'll get up a few more events. Boxing it is.'

The two barmen went at that, for they were known for
having bouts above. They gave it some welly, and the older
one knocked the younger clean out, and a good few teeth
as well.

Then somebody said they wanted to see Sid at it, but
he said he wasn't stirring, and they may find him something
he could do sitting down. So Budd plonked down beside
him and said it was arm-wrestling.

Well that gave a smile to all, but good man Sid, he said
he'd go for it. And to give him his due, the two men never
left twelve o'clock for a good few minutes, though you
could see the veins bulging black in their arms. But Sid

hadn't the strength of Budd, and both men knew he would tire, so Sid relaxed the grip all of a sudden, which surprised Budd that much he did the same, and then Sid was all ready with a big push to slam him down. Some trickster. He got him within an inch of the table, all heads down around it to see was it touching. But Budd pumped up the muscles and inch by inch he raised him back up to due north and then down the other side. But now Sid held him there, grunting and snorting, and if he didn't start to inch him back up. Well, Achill stepped in then and called it a dead heat.

'We need have neither of you pair ruin your trigger hands for a bit of sport. The same prize for both men.'

And they took five bundles of twenties each, a cool thousand cash.

Running next, and Sid and Budd still had power in their legs at least, and a graw to beat the other, for both stood up, along with young Anthony again. They were off, with Budd taking an early lead round the first bend, but Sid was in tight behind him, Budd could nearly feel the man's breath between his shoulder blades, that close he ran, all the way around the pub till they skirted the farm. And there it was that Budd put his right foot in a fat cowpat and went on his arse in the shite, so that Sid crossed the line ahead of him, though Budd was back on his heels and a close second, spitting out lumps of dung and straw. 'That man Sid. Even the cows take his side. I swear to God.' And another good laugh was had.

Anthony took last place with good grace.

'The only man who could beat Sid, though he's far from the youngest here, is Achill himself, the best sprinter among us.'

Achill opened his own wallet and gave him five twenties for that.

The men called out for one more event, the throwing. Pig and Merrion stepped up, but Achill hushed them, knowing what it would likely turn into. Not today, thank you.

'The only man here who hasn't a prize, and well deserves one, is Pig himself. He'd bate the lot of us any time he chose. So let you take the honours, Pig, but hand them on to Merrion, like the boss man should, thinking only of the men under him, and nothing of himself.'

Pig nodded his fat head, and did just what Achill said.

Because, what else do you do?

86

A wee crack of light was on the horizon when they all started drifting home. There was some twangy country shite playing, and them stumbling around trying to find coats and keys.

'Nobody's to drive,' says Sid. 'I'm giving lifts.'

There was only Achill left in the place. And now he was on his own, he let rip his grief. The face crumpled up, and big heavy sobs came rolling out of him. Choking and wailing. The gasps and the snotters. Retching and shuddering. The whole thing. Now he'd started, he couldn't stop.

He'd get up now and again and into the jacks and try and piss on Henry, but he had nothing in him. So he hoiked the body out of the gutter and gave it a kicking. But he was too tired to do any damage. In spite of the dragging and the bullets and the beatings, the man still looked like himself.

87

Words were being had, at the highest level. They'd kept the details off the news so far, but only just, by threatening head honchos with dirt-digging in the tabloids and big cuts in the next Budget, and then buttering them up with promises of future gongs.

But the army were champing at the bit. As far as they were concerned, this meant war. They were going to get the body back, hell or high water.

The unionists were up in arms too. Our friend in particular. Mr Paul Bright.

Strings were pulled in Whitehall. It found its way to the top. And I mean the very top.

'Relax, Mr Bright. I have someone on the ground who owes me a favour.'

London had her notified. The wee secretary Iris sent word, for she knew just where to find her. And the woman called in on the same number, got put through in the very same way.

'This is Theresa. I have nothing to say to you, but.'

'Really? Then allow me. You owe me, I believe was the phrase.'

'Fuck you. I'm not in the mood the night. And I think you'll find we're quits.'

'Under the circumstances, given how things have played out, my view is that the price paid has been a little higher than anticipated. After this, let's agree we're all square.'

'You're asking an awful lot.'

'You misunderstand me, my dear lady. This isn't a request. It's an order.'

So down she drove again to the Ships, to see her own wee boy.

'Can you not eat something, or take a rest? Will I not come in for the night and keep you company? A woman's body is great cure for all ills. You should try and enjoy whatever of life is left, for a man like you might not have long.

'But one way or another, you have to give back that dead soldier. It's not right. It's not natural. I'm hearing it's causing all kinds of ructions. Think of the poor man's family, the grief you're putting them through. Let them say their good-byes, the same as you have yourself. You can't live your whole life in fury.'

'You were sent, weren't you?'

'Whether I was or I wasn't, this is what has to happen.'

He thought about it. It was finished. He didn't actually give a fuck any more.

'If it has to, then it has to. But I'll not shift. Let them come and get him.'

88

The call came back through to Iris, while she was taking five, munching at a tray bake. She dusted the crumbs off her skirt and went right away, leaving the bun half ate.

In to Bernard, sitting there among them, the ruin of the last night's disco.

He looked shocking. He hadn't shaved. Like filth round his neck and his face, as if he'd smeared on black ash from the grate.

'Sir. A message from London.'

He squinted at the paper, shook his head.

'I can't focus. Tell me what they want.'

'You're to go and get the body back, sir. Someone from the Det will get you over the border, and up to the pub where O'Brien has him.'

'That's their plan, is it? I ask politely for the corpse, and because he's a wise, thoughtful, moral individual, he hands it over out of the goodness of his heart?'

'I think that's the idea, sir.'

'Brilliant. The sheer calibre of our civil service never ceases to astonish.'

But he did his duty. Lifted the phone, to Henry's mother.

'It's Bernard. How are you bearing up?'

'I'm not. It's unbearable.'

'They've asked me to cross the border and recover the body.'

'From whom, exactly?'

'From his killer.'

'You're quite mad. At least bring me with you. Do you know what I'll do? I'll take out his liver and eat it in front of him. That's how I feel right now. Do you understand?'

'The orders are quite clear. I simply felt it my duty to inform you. It may well be a set-up, and I'll take that chance. I have a little fire in my belly still. Probably one more fight left in me, if it comes to it. And if that's my fate, so be it.'

Polly heard him kitting out, and tapped at the door with a couple of other officers.

'Sir, we're not sure this is a good idea.'

The sight of him, smiling his smug wee smile, and something in the old man snapped.

'You know what's a fucking good idea? If any one of you conducts yourself with half of the courage and intelligence of that man. None of you has a sliver of his character. I watched you last night. Heroes of the dance floor. Taking advantage of young girls, who ought to be at school, shipped in here to satisfy your egos. You should be ashamed. I am.'

89

On the road, Bernard saw a torch, circling. His stomach turned over. Hair on his arms prickled. Senior officers had a good record in the conflict, but there had been exceptions. They'd love one more for their collection.

The voice at the window was local.

'Where are you off to at this time of night? Have you no fear of the Ra?'

'You make a damn good point.'

'Did you not hear what's happened? One of your top men is down.'

'You're very well informed.'

'I watched the same fella over the years. I used to be involved, though Achill bade me not fight lately, for he wouldn't himself, but we used to marvel at the fierce goes of your man. It's all gearing up now again, for they've no patience with ceasefires at all.'

'If you're one of his, then is the body still there? Or is it too late?'

'He's still in one piece. Come on and I'll take you in. No one'll bother you, with me by your side. Shift over there, and I'll drive.'

They passed over the border, through another couple of IVCPs. Waved on.

In they pulled at the Ships. The driver took his hand. A different voice now. English.

'I'm in deep. One of London's. I can't risk being seen inside with you. But I wish you well. Remind him of his own father, that's my advice. All he has.'

The man left him there, parked by the door.

He heard the music and laughing from inside. Stepped out. Pulled open the door.

Achill was sitting there with two others, finishing a bite to eat. The rest of the squad were standing about, the ones that couldn't sleep, back up again for more. One by one they hushed when they saw him. He was in civvies, but they knew by the hair. By the cut of his jib.

Bernard recognised his man too, but made out like he hadn't.

'I'm looking for Mr O'Brien.'

He was told to wait. Anthony went over and whispered in Achill's ear.

A nod. He was brought over and offered a seat. He took it.

Achill said nothing. Didn't look up.

'I won't beat about the bush. First and foremost, I've come to pay tribute to you and your men. You're a fine foe for an old soldier. I admire your skills, and your grit, and your ruthlessness. I'd be proud to have any of you serve under me. What you've achieved, in military terms, operating entirely in secret, is quite astonishing. It speaks highly of your commitment to your cause. And I don't begrudge you that, not at all. After four tours, the only thing I know for certain is that if I'd grown up in West Belfast or South Armagh or the Bogside, I'd certainly have joined the IRA.'

'Enough. Tell me your true business.'

'Yes, quite right. I expect you can guess. I've come to ask for him back.'

Bernard stood, and then he kicked at a spot on the floor, scattering the fag butts. He pinched up his trousers and knelt.

He took Achill's hand in his own. He touched his lips to the knuckles.

That cleared the place, fast.

Just him and Achill now. He stayed down.

The breath in and out of him. Achill too. Nothing but that.

'Please. I can't do any more. I don't think a British officer has ever before kissed the hand of the man who killed his best soldier. Please. Think of your own father, and the great joy it brings him to hear you're alive. Please. This man was like a son to me. He has a mother, and a wife, and a child. They all need to know. Please. They need him back.'

Achill pushed the man away, but not hard. He was thinking now again of his own da.

He knelt down beside, like the child he still was, some-where under it all. The family rosary. Confessions. Sunday Mass with his da. Praying hard to be half the man he was.

Before he knew what, he was weeping again.

Bernard listened as long as he could. But then he went.

Each of them. The both of them. If you could have seen.

The long howls of them. You could hear them up the stairs.

You could hear them in the road, is the truth. The men standing around.

But nobody said a thing. Just like as if it wasn't happening. See nothing, hear nothing. Say nothing.

90

When they were done, Achill stood, and hauled Bernard up too.

'You're a decent man to come out here on your own. Balls of iron too. So come and sit down at this table here and listen to what I'm going to tell you.

'My da has no soldiers to command, just one stubborn bastard of a son who's going into the ground before he does. But your country brought this on yourselves, so quit your gurning. All your crying won't bring your best officer back, and if I was that bothered about my da, I wouldn't be here, I'd be there with him. And I tell you this, things are going to get worse before they get better. We can't get rid of our grief, neither one of us, so let's leave it there on the floor, for it does us no good. But there's no way out of it either, for life is nothing only grief. Are you listening? I said come here and sit down.'

'I don't want to sit down. I want to take what I came for and get out of here fast.'

A few wee spits of the old fury now, dancing in Achill's eyes.

'Listen here. Don't piss me off, old man. I know rightly you had some help getting this length, and nobody would raise an eyebrow if you met with a wee accident on your way home. I could plug you yet.'

So Bernard sat and took a drink. Scotch. Achill had the same. The two men toasted each other with a wee nod, and each other's dead.

'You'll eat with me before you head. Napoleon always said an army marches on its stomach. It's right to fast at the right time, but there's no shame in feeding again when that time is over. Save the tears for when you have him home.'

Inside in the kitchen, Achill cooked the food himself. He did it lovely, just how Pat always did for him. He hadn't forgot.

When it was in the oven, he ducked out the door and ran round the side, where the others were huddled.

'Get in there and lift that body out of the bogs and give it a scrub, carbolic soap or whatever will get rid of the smell of piss. Dress it up in my good suit here, and get it in the boot of his car before he sees it, for that might snap him altogether. If he has a go at me he'll come off worse, and I don't want that business on top of what's already happened.'

Then he blessed himself and said a wee prayer to Pat, that he hoped he didn't mind the body going back. In he went again to Bernard. He told him it was in the car already and he could inspect it in the morning. And now it was time to eat.

When that was done, they just looked, each taking the other in, for they never had the chance before, sat in the quiet, at close quarters.

Michael Hughes

They saw the whole thing. They each carried every bit of it with them.

It was the Englishman that spoke first.

'I haven't slept since he died, and I need to lie down before I dare drive.'

'There's rooms ready made up above. But, here. Would you mind sleeping in the car? If any of the rest of the squad see you upstairs, word might reach Pig, and if he gets wind of you sleeping here then we'll be back to square one. But one more thing I'll do for you. Tell me when his funeral is to be, and I'll make sure there's nothing until after.'

'A fortnight or so, once everything is organised.'

'That I'll do, no bother. All will be quiet till it's over, in his honour.'

91

Bernard was asleep in seconds, but it was an uneasy rest. In his dream, the same Det man who drove came and woke him in a hurry, saying Shane Campbell had found out he was there. He woke in a hot sweat, tangled in his coat.

Nothing. Dead country silence. But the dream was too close to the facts for comfort.

He started the car and away.

92

Henry's funeral was long, and tough. Dress uniforms. The Last Post. Cameras poking their noses in. Max wailing to be picked up. Anna dizzy with exhaustion. Just get it over with. Please God, don't let it be over yet.

After, they sat up in the kitchen at Holland Park, coats still on, drinking tea. They spoke a bit, murmurs now and again of who would arrange what, but mostly they just sat. No one dared call a car, for they knew when this day ended, the war would go on.

So they sat. Trying to think it all out. Trying hard to believe it was for the best.

Some day, they knew, the string would be pulled to stop it all. Not yet. When all the pieces were in place. The higher-ups would settle it, find the middle course.

Until then, we live and die here below. One nod of the head, one tip of the scales.

The way it always was.

The way it has to be.